THE VENOM OF VANQUISH

THE VENOM OF VANQUISH
VANQUISH TRILOGY

DAVID LEE STONE

Copyright © 2022 David Lee Stone

First published in Great Britain in 2006
by Hodder Children's Books.

This revised edition
published in 2022 by Kingsbrook Publishing.

All rights reserved. Apart from any use permitted under UK copyright law, this publication may only be reproduced, stored or transmitted, in any form, or by any means with prior permission in writing from the publishers or in the case of reprographic production in accordance with the terms of licences issued by the Copyright Licensing Agency and may not be otherwise circulated in any form of binding or cover other than that in which it is published and without a similar condition being imposed on the subsequent purchaser. All characters in this publication are fictitious and any resemblance to real personas, living or dead, is purely coincidental.

A Catalogue record for this book is available
from the British Library.

ISBN: 978-1-7397776-3-0

The right of David Lee Stone to be identified as author of this work has been asserted in accordance with sections 77 and 78 of the Copyright Designs and Patents Act 1988

Printed and bound in Great Britain by
Clays Ltd, Elcograf S.p.A.

For Evangeline Lilly Rose Stone

DRAMATIS PERSONAE

- Banks, Rumlink (undead human), *assassin*
- Burnie (troglodyte), *chair of the Dullitch council*
- Cadrick, Taciturn (human), *Council vice chairman*
- Diveall, Sorrell (human), *sorcerer, noble lord*
- Franklin, Victor (human), *assassin*
- Goldaxe, Gordo (dwarf), *mercenary, guard captain*
- Green, Mifkindle (human), *assassin*
- Lambontroff, Loogie (decapitated human head), *rogue*
- Lye, Rin (human), *senior judge*
- Lythay, Vortas (human), *a poisoner*
- Nazz (ogre), *mercenary*
- Obegarde, Jareth (vampire), *consulting detective*
- Quickstint, Jimmy (human), *gravedigger/thief*
- Reish, Colonel (human), *soldier/officer*
- Ripple, Rorgrim (human), *owner of the Rotting Ferret Inn*
- Shably, Brim (human), *senior guard*

- Spatula, Effigy (human), *agitator/freedom fighter*
- Stanhope (human), *palace guard*
- Teethgrit, Gape (human), *barbarian mercenary*
- Teethgrit, Groan (human), *barbarian mercenary*

Note for New Readers

In the previous volume of the Illmoor Chronicles, Viscount Curfew, Lord of Dullitch, was kidnapped by a ruthless sorcerer named Sorrell Diveal. The kidnap, though brilliantly executed, was eventually foiled by a valiant team of Dullitch citizens, and Viscount Curfew was subsequently returned to his throne...

PROLOGUE

'A cave dragon, Gordo! It's an actual, fire-breathing cave dragon!'

'I know THAT, idiot: the damn thing just cost me half a head of hair!'

'What're we going to do, then?'

'Just keep running!'

Gape Teethgrit and Gordo Goldeaxe thundered down the tunnels as though the hounds of hell were after them. In truth, the thing pursuing them was a good deal worse and would probably have eaten the hounds of hell for breakfast, or possibly even as a snack *before* breakfast.

Cave dragons were known for their great appetite.

'Hang on!' Gape yelled, grabbing hold of a torch-mount to stop himself. 'Where's Groan?'

'What do you mean "where's Groan"?' Gordo slowed his own progress in stages: fast waddle gave way to a waddle, finally degenerating into the staggered amble that Gape recognised. 'I thought he was behind us!'

'He was!'

'Great...' The dwarf squinted into the darkness. 'We must have lost him at that last junction. Oh well, I don't doubt he'll find his way out....'

THUMP.

The corridor shook; Gordo and Gape both struggled to keep their footing.

'Rrruuunnn!'

Gape dashed up the corridor, disappearing into the shadowy murk.

The dwarf sighed. Then he stashed his battleaxe on its assigned shoulder strap, summoned up a last reserve of energy...and stopped dead. Gape had re-emerged from the gloom. He was carrying an enormous golden shield.

'What're you doing? I told you to run!'

'I did run: straight into a wall. There's a dead-end, up there. I did find this shield, though.'

THUMP.

The tunnel rocked again, but this time the duo managed to stand their ground.

'A cave dragon, eh?' the barbarian muttered. 'How big are they, generally speaking?'

Gordo shrugged. 'About eight metres, give or take.'

'And the one that's chasing us?'

'Oh, I don't know: about ten, maybe?'

'Do you think we can take it?'

The dwarf stared up at his companion, just to see if he was serious.

'You're joking, right?'

'Well, I was just wondering-'

'No, Gape. I do not think we can take it.'

'Not even a chance?'

'No, not even one-eighth of half a quarter's chance. It can

breathe fire every few minutes, not to mention the fact that it can also do considerable damage with its claws.'

Gape drew in a breath, then looked up suddenly.

'What if we had a three-metre dragon-killing war-axe?' he asked.

Gordo boggled at him.

'*Do* we have a three-metre dragon-killing war-axe?'

'No.'

Then what in the name of sanity did you ask for?'

'LOOK! IT'S GROAN!'

The giant barbarian had appeared from the mouth of the cave that bled into the far end of the tunnel. He was running towards them at a remarkable speed for such a big man, leaping boulders and sidestepping spear traps that sprang from the walls on both sides.

As he reached a point approximately halfway between the cave mouth and his companions, the walls behind him collapsed to reveal the group's gargantuan pursuer.

The cave dragon lumbered forward, its impossible bulk threatening the integrity of the cave system in which it had lain, undisturbed, for more than a hundred years. Enraged at the interruption, it marched on, stopping only to lower its massive head and release a jet of flame at its prey.

Groan dived for the tunnel floor, completing an awkward forward roll before he managed to get himself back on his feet.

'Do something!' Gordo screamed at the barbarian's long-haired brother. 'Before we all end up grilled!'

Gape looked around desperately.

'Why can't YOU do something?' he snapped at the dwarf. 'I thought your lot knew a thing or two about handling dragons!'

'We do,' Gordo yelled back. 'We know enough not to go near them! Now, are you going to use one of those enchanted swords or am I going to have to throw YOU at it?'

Gape glanced from Gordo to the weapon in his hand, and back.

'I can't just throw it and hope-'

'Of course you can! They come back on command, don't they?'

'Yes, but-'

'Well then, you get another chance if you mess it up. Now, THROW THE DAMN THING.'

Gape nodded, then reeled back and hurled the sword at the beast's chest: the dragon let out a defiant roar and took another step forward.

'Good work,' Gordo mumbled. 'Now you've *really* upset it.'

'You told me to throw the sword!'

'Yeah, well – I was wrong!' Gordo drew his battleaxe from the strap on his shoulder and hefted it in both hands. 'Right – my turn!'

The dwarf waddle-charged his way up the tunnel, hurrying around Groan en route to the dragon. Arriving beneath it, he swung the battleaxe round in a wide arc and cut deep into one of its scaly legs.

The beast gave a roar of disapproval, then drove the enormous appendage forward, sending Gordo on a flight back up the tunnel and propelling his axe into the earthy ceiling of the corridor.

'Argh,' Gordo managed, trying to get to his feet again. He'd landed badly, and he could feel the beginnings of an intense pain in his ribs. 'Wh-where's my battleaxe?'

'In the roof,' said Gape. 'Nice try, though.'

The two companions peered back up the corridor. It seemed that although Gordo's offensive may have been entirely ineffectual, it had bought Groan a few vital seconds. The giant warrior jumped to his feet, pounded along the tunnel and came to a halt, puffing and panting, before the pair.

'I 'ate drag'ns,' he boomed, raising a hand to his forehead. 'Got me 'brows ag'in: took a fortnight ta grow 'em back las' time.'

'Tell me about it,' Gordo bleated. 'I left my helmet back at the portcullis and the damn thing scorched half my hair off. Gape seems to have escaped its attention, so far.'

THUMP.

The dragon demolished another section of the tunnel in its quest to get at the trio.

'What're we going to do?' Gape snapped at the dwarf. 'I've only got one sword left!'

'Call the other one back, then!'

'I can't: it must be embedded too deep!'

'Ah, you're useless, you are!'

'Ha! I didn't see you doing much better, gnome-features! Your axe is still in the roof!'

'Why, you...'

'I could try 'n' knock it out.'

Both warriors turned to regard Groan, who was rubbing his chin thoughtfully.

'What with?' Gordo yelled. 'There aren't any *trees* around...'

'Wiv me fist.'

'Oh, you can't be serious.'

'He is,' said Gape.

''Ere,' Groan rumbled, turning to his brother. 'Gimme that plate.'

'It's not a plate, Groan: it's a shield.'

'Whatever.'

Groan took the golden shield. Then he turned around and walked purposefully towards the oncoming nightmare.

'He's insane!' Gordo snapped, turning back to Gape. 'I never had much doubt, but this proves it. He's absolutely out of his mind.'

The barbarian nodded in agreement.

'Well?' Gordo exclaimed, rounding on him. 'Are you just going to stand there and let your brother die? Are you?'

Gape pursed his lips. 'Rather than face a cave dragon, you mean? Hmm...actually, yes, I think I might.'

'Throw the other sword!'

'But I didn't get the last one back!'

Gordo rolled his eyes. 'And? You're not exactly going to need it where *you're* going, are you?'

Gape thought for a moment, then shrugged and hurled the second blade at the dragon. It turned over and over in the air, finally landing in the beast's scaly neck.

The dragon let out another roar of annoyance, and then released a second fire-stream that quickly engulfed the entire corridor.

'Argghhhhh!'

Flesh singed and armour blackened, Gape and Gordo quickly recovered their footing and glared back into the blast zone. Groan was still standing, the enormous shield raised high above his head. Moreover, the dragon was studying the shield with an air of interest.

'Do you think it's a magic shield?' Gape wondered aloud.

'Could be,' Gordo admitted. 'Look: it's bending its head to have a closer look!'

The dragon craned down to study its distorted reflection in the shiny gold shield. *The gold shield that was shiny...and gold, with shiny bits that made the gold bits look even more shiny...and gold.*

The dragon was momentarily entranced.

But Groan wasn't: he waited until he could feel the beast's fiery breath upon him, then he swung the shield around with all his might, moving like a discus thrower, and let go.

There was a resoundingly dull CLANG.

And the beast collapsed.

Unfortunately, half the corridor fell in with it. The sound was deafening.

As the smoke and dust cleared, Gape and Gordo carefully approached the sleeping giant.

'G-groan?' Gordo called, his voice edged with worry. 'Are you OK?'

'Say something if you can hear us!' Gape added, feeling guilty that he was secretly more concerned about retrieving his swords.

'Mmmf,' said a voice.

'Groan? Is that you?'

'Yeah. 'S me.'

'Where are you?'

'I'm under 'ere.'

'Are you all right?'

There was a moment of silence. Then the voice said: 'Nah, 'm under a plate, under a drag'n. I ain't 'appy.'

Gordo looked round at the barbarian's brother.

'Gape! Leave those swords alone and GET back here this

minute. We've got to lift this dragon's head!'

'What about your axe?'

Gordo looked up, thoughtfully. Then he said: 'Groan, can you breathe under there?'

'Yeah - bit.'

The dwarf nodded.

'All right, Gape: get the weapons first. Then we'll lift the dragon's head. We're not killing it, mind: it's very bad luck to kill a dragon. Groan will tell you that.'

THE PAGE HURRIED through the dusty halls of Phlegm Keep and arrived, exasperated, in the Chamber of Elders. All four of the wizened old men looked up at the boy, their crusty eyebrows raised.

'Yes?' said one, inquisitively.

'I-it's the King, sirs. He's gone, and he's taken the Captain of the Guard with him!'

The elders glanced at each other before the first one rediscovered his voice. 'Gone, you say? Gone *where*, exactly?'

The page shrugged.

'Not sure, sirs: no one had seen him for weeks, so we plucked up the courage to break into his private apartments. We found *this* nailed to the throne, but I haven't opened it.'

The boy allowed himself a cough, then removed a sealed scrap of parchment from his jerkin. 'Do you want to examine it privately or should I read it out...?'

The first elder gave a dismissive wave of his hand, but the rest looked at the page expectantly.

'Right,' said the boy, swallowing. 'It says: THE FOLLOWING NOTE WAS DICTATED BY HIS MAJESTY

GROAN TEETHGRIT THE FIRST, TO CAPTAIN GORDO GOLDEAXE: 'AVE GONE TO THE BOMA CAVES TO GET AN 'AMMER F'R THE SHELF. GORDO TOO. BACK IN SIX WEEKS. THE KING. PS. WE 'AVEN'T TAKEN LOOGIE WIV US, AS I'M LEAVIN' 'IM 'N CHARGE. ALL RIGHT, THASSIT NOW YA CAN CHUCK THE QUILL AW...'

The elders glanced at one another: one looked confused and one looked angry, but they all looked very tired. Eventually, one said:

'But I don't understand it: we've got *thousands* of hammers *here*!'

'And he's left Loogie Lambontroff, *a reanimated human head*, in control of the Kingdom,' another remarked.

'That's outrageous! Where is the infant prince?'

'If I may remind you, sirs, King Groan sent his son away to Legrash at the beginning of the year.'

'And the Qu...I mean, the King's consort?'

The page smiled weakly.

'She was sent into exile last month, sir, remember? After that business where she kissed the palace guard...'

The elder frowned.

'She kissed a palace guard? What, really? Which one?'

'Um...all of them, I think, sir.'

There was some intense muttering.

'Getting back to the matter in hand...' said another elder, stroking his wisp of beard and eyeing the page with dread. 'Where is, er, our temporary sovereign now?'

'The throne room, sir.'

'You actually took it to the throne room! How did you know to do that if you've only just read the note?'

'The head: it er...informed me itself, sir.'

'Tell me you've not put it on the throne...'

'Well, as a matter of fact-'

'Are you insane, boy? Are you actually mad?'

The page looked wretched.

'I didn't know what to do, sir! TheKing left it on a shelf in his private quarters and it had been there for weeks! I tell you, sir, it was livid! It threatened all sorts if I didn't put it straight on the throne!'

The elder sighed.

'It's a decapitated head, boy. What's it going to do, spit on you?'

'If I may just interrupt,' said his colleague. 'What exactly did Loogie say?'

'It *demanded* that I put it on the throne immediately, sir, as per the King's instructions.'

The first elder put his head in his hands and sobbed.

'Fantastic,' said his wispy-bearded colleague. 'Not only are we ruled by a muscle-bound idiot and his dwarf cohort, *now* we've got a decapitated head playing king while they're away. I tell you, this city has gone right to the dogs...'

THE UNCONSCIOUS DRAGON was still an immensely bulky shape in the background as Gordo's stubby fingers felt along the wall for any signs of a lever. He soon found what he was looking for – a tiny finger-pull, obscured by dust and dirt. He pulled it back slightly, heard an audible 'click' and turned, smiling, to his companions

'You see? A secret door,' he said, indicating the wall section as it slid noisily aside. 'You've got a lot to learn about dungeons, Gape. NEVER leave a dead-end without checking for secret doors. Isn't that right, Groan?'

'Yeah,' said Groan, who was still covered in dragon-spit from his earlier escapade. 'Dungeons is full of 'em.'

'Ahah!' Gordo exclaimed, peering into the chamber beyond. 'Boys, I think we've found it! Gape, grab that torch and give it to me: you can keep a lookout while we go in.'

Looking back over recent events, the mercenary band had fought long and hard to reach their prize. They had braved many perils, wandered both night and day, fought goblins, werewolves, demons, zombies, and even cave dragons. They'd delved into the darkest, dankest tunnels of Illmoor and, now, in the very bowels of the Boma Cave system, they had found what they were looking for...

The hammer - for such a thing it was, hovered above a fractured plinth, causing the air around it to hum.

Groan sat perched on a heavy rock, sharpening the business end of his broadsword, while his dwarf counterpart shuffled towards the plinth. Then, bringing the burning torch as close as his courage would allow, Gordo attempted to examine the plaque beneath it.

'This thing is ancient,' he whispered. 'The sign is in Troddish.'

'Can't you turn it the uvver way up?' asked Groan, frowning.

Gordo sighed: he'd tried many times to imagine the workings of Groan's mind, but somehow he'd always drawn a blank.

'Troddish,' he patiently explained, 'is the language they speak in distant Trod. It doesn't mean 'upside down'.'

The big barbarian scratched his cannonball head.

'Is Trod that place where mushrooms come from?'

'Er...yes,' lied Gordo, to avoid a more intricate conversation. 'That's right.'

'Ahh...Gape went over there for a bit; he ended up killin' the same goblin 'at did for his uncle's backache.'

The dwarf nodded, but his brain managed to edit Groan's words and salvage a workable idea.

'GAPE!' he shouted at the secret door.

For a moment, there was silence. Then a head poked around the entrance: it had lots of hair attached to it.

'You called, o' short, helmeted one?'

Gordo rolled his eyes: there were no words for just how much he *hated* Groan's anvil-chinned brother.

'Don't bother with the lookout thing: there's nobody down here but us. Listen, can you read Troddish?'

'Can I read it?' The hairy barbarian cracked off a riotous laugh. 'Ha! It's like a second language to me!'

'Fantastic. What does this sign say, please?'

Groan had continued to sharpen his blade. 'I bet it says 'stuff off or die',' he muttered. 'They *all* say that.'

'Actually,' Gape countered, having vaulted across the cavern and snatched the torch from Gordo, 'It says: Behold: You Stand And Witness The Very Hammer of Romith-seth-athrith-amothroth Adegrataray.'

'That was his name?' Gordo exclaimed. 'No wonder they never put his statue up: the engraving 'd take a fortnight...'

'I haven't finished,' Gape snapped. 'It goes on to say that Romith-seth-athrith-amothroth Adegrataray was the son of the legendary giant-killer, Ramith-soth-ekrith-onoronrith Adegrataray, and grandson of Bobova Thursdy.'

'Bobova Thursdy?' echoed the dwarf, a smile cracking his face. 'That name's a bit different from the other two, isn't it?'

'I know,' Gape agreed. 'They weren't too proud of the granddad, by all accounts. It certainly doesn't have much about him on here: just says he grew things. In fact, they must've *really* hated him – his picture's been completely vandalised.'

'Maybe he named 'em boaf,' said Groan, thoughtfully.

'You could be right,' Gordo conceded. 'So it doesn't say anything about a curse or a trap or certain death?'

Gape shook his head.

'No: nothing like that. It's quite boring, as signs go.'

Gordo suddenly squinted at the plaque.

'What about the scrawly bit at the bottom? Did you read that? It says, er, 'Ikmick ruybyelick moosti uf nase, marmarik'.'

'Does it?'

Gape pursed his lips as he tried to decipher the message in his head.

'That means: don't blow smoke in my face, Sally.'

Gordo removed his helmet and scratched his bushy eyebrows.

'Why would they put that on a plinth in a dungeon cavern?' he said.

'Maybe she was smokin' in 'ere,' said Groan.

The others stared at him.

'Who?'

'Sally.'

'There *is* no Sally, Groan,' the dwarf replied. 'Gape must've translated it wrong. The cavern that we're all standing in is more than three *thousand* years old. Do you understand how ancient that makes it?'

Groan thought of an answer, but Gordo cut him off before he could voice it. 'This cavern's damn near as old as Illmoor itself!'

Gape nodded.

'So should we take the hammer or not?' he asked, a little

bewildered.

'Come to that, what has the hammer got to do with everything else? And why do we need it, again? Sorry – I'm totally lost, here.'

'Don't you ever listen?' Gordo snapped. 'This is the thing we've been hunting for over a month: the actual, real, one and only hammer used to put up the Sacred Shelf of Medamichi.'

'It is?'

'YES.'

'Fine,' Gape mouthed, sucking in his bottom lip. 'And what exactly *is* the Sacred Shelf of Medamichi?'

'It's the mountain shelf that the city of Dullitch was originally built on!'

Gape considered this for a moment, and then appeared to reach a conclusion.

'That's the biggest load of old pants I ever heard in my life!'

'You what?' Gordo exclaimed. 'Is that all the respect you've got to show for the greatest find in the history of Illmoor? We've braved hell and high water for this!'

'Well, I mean look at it! You couldn't put up a picture frame with that hammer...'

'That's not the point, is it?' Gordo screamed. 'The *point* is that just about every member of the Illmoor nobility believes in it. Not only that, but they know what this thing looks like, and they'll pay through the nose for it. I'm telling you we'll scoop an absolute fortune in trade deals once Lord Curfew finds out that we've recovered it. What's more, the hammer is rumoured to be a key to the Ultimate Treasure of Illmoor.'

'Have you read the wall, yet?'

'Mmm?' Gordo followed Gape's pointed finger. There, on

the east wall of the cave, was a passage of elaborate text.

'How could *I* read it? It's in Trod, again!'

Gape shrugged.

'Then I will,' he said, ambling up to the wall and squinting at the message. 'It says: Prophecy holds, that in the Year of Stormtides, one who was long thought lost will return as a servant of evil. Vanquish, lord of all darkness, will send forth this emissary to take The City. The servant, of noble blood but denied the throne, will be possessed of arcane power and will stop at nothing to rule. He will do this by way of a clever deception and the good will not *see* him. Understand that He must never find the Hammer, for with it He may unlock the secret and free the abomination that his evil master hath become. Thus writes the Last Keeper of the Hammer, Romith Adegrataray.'

Gape turned back to the dwarf and smiled. 'Do you think by 'the City' it means Dullitch?'

'Of course;' said Gordo, nodding. 'These old prophecies are *always* about the capital. 'But it doesn't matter, because it's wrong.'

'Why would you say that?'

'Well, Stormtides was last year; we're on Moontides now and, anyway, I'm pretty sure that we'd know if Dullitch had fallen to an evil sorcerer. I mean, Viscount Curfew's a damn nuisance, but he's no-'

Gordo stopped in mid-sentence, partly because he'd forgotten what he was talking about, but mostly because he'd just seen Groan stride up to the plinth and snatch the hammer out of the air

'Mmm...nuffing's 'appened,' said the barbarian, dismissively, handing the sacred tool to Gordo.

Then the first rock fell.

CHAPTER
ONE

It was gently stroking midnight at Dullitch Palace when Viscount Curfew came thundering out of the throne room as if he was on fire.

The taller of the two chamber sentries (who'd been slumped at their posts, half asleep) hardly had time to blink before the viscount snatched him viciously by the throat.

'The painting: the one in my room! What's behind it? Answer me, damn you! Answer me now!'

The guard choked and spluttered as his colleague, who'd luckily escaped Curfew's first attentions, made a brave attempt to speak on his behalf.

'Y-you mean your self-portrait, my lord?'

Curfew rounded on him like the wrath of gods, shoving the other sentry back against the wall.

'Who are you?'

'Shably, Excellency: Senior Guard Shably.'

'*You* know what's behind the portrait, do you?'

'Yes, my lord.' Shably nodded, but something about the viscount's expression advised him to take a step back. 'It's an escape tunnel. You ordered it to be built just before you were kidnapped: don't you remember?'

Curfew all but snarled with malice.

'You know where it escapes to?' he demanded.

'Yes, my lord. It runs out to the back of the Summer Gardens. If-'

'Follow me now, both of you.'

The viscount turned and bolted off down the corridor. 'Bring your swords!' he screamed back.

The two guards shared a brief and very worried glance before hurrying after the ruling lord of Dullitch.

IN ALL HIS years at the palace, Brim Shably had never seen Curfew run at such a pace. As he dashed after the viscount, he cursed himself for his shortcomings: evidently, there had been a major breach of security on his watch. *But*, he thought, *how could an interloper breach the secret tunnel? Wasn't there a guard posted beside the entrance at all times? Moreover, wasn't Private Stanhope stationed inside the tunnel every evening to watch for intruders? What was going on?*

Shably arrived, out of breath, on the fringe of the Summer Gardens, his colleague still some distance behind him. Noting Curfew's enraged expression, he quickly pointed out the disguised wall section that contained the secret door to the tunnel. Thankfully, there was a stout guard on duty beside it. Shably managed a smile and was just about to push his luck with a sigh of relief when Curfew seized his sword, strode up to the wall-guard and put the blade against the shocked man's throat. 'Who's in there?' he screamed, tightening his grip on the weapon. 'Who's in the tunnel?'

'Answer him!' Shably added, suddenly afraid for the man.

'Only Private Stanhope, my lord,' the wall-guard managed, his eyes watering up. 'He's watching your end of the tunnel for intruders.'

'Is he still in there?' Curfew spat, twisting the sword edge so that it began to draw blood from the stunned guard's neck. It was Shably who answered the question:

'He would be in there, my lord. From nine o'clock each night, as per your instructions.'

Curfew turned his head slightly.

'Is it always him, or do others have this job?'

'Always Stanhope, my lord,' Shably said, wincing as he saw the wall-guard's pained expression. 'You personally selected him for the job, remember?'

Curfew suddenly withdrew the sword and took a step back. As he did so, the wall-guard practically collapsed with relief.

'Call him out,' the viscount muttered. 'My lord?'

Curfew took a measured breath, as if he were trying to subdue his temper.

'Call him out, Mr Shably...while you still have the privilege of being a palace guard.'

It was at this point that Shably's ageing sentry-partner arrived in the gardens.

'No time to rest!' the senior guard advised him. 'Get into the tunnel and tell Stanhope to-'

'NO!'

All eyes turned back to Curfew, who was now virtually unrecognisable from the mild-mannered man most of the guards were used to.

'Nobody goes in there. I want you, Shably, to *call him out.*'

The guard master ignored the baffled looks of his inferiors and nodded obediently. Then he stepped forward, felt for the hidden catch and triggered the well-oiled mechanism that dutifully sprang the secret door.

'STANHOPE!' he called up the tunnel. 'PRIVATE STANHOPE, GET DOWN HERE IMMEDIATELY.'

There followed a few moments of awkward silence before footsteps drew close. Slowly and very cautiously, Stanhope emerged from the tunnel. He was a thin man, ghost-white and shaking to point of insanity. As his eyes met those of Viscount Curfew, he raised an accusatory finger and tried to speak, but the words, it seemed, would not come.

'Step away from this man,' the viscount instructed, raising Shably's sword.

'Y-you!' Private Stanhope managed, finally finding enough of his voice to serve him. 'Y-you're...'

There was a sudden, swish of air and to the absolute astonishment of the gathered guards, Private Stanhope was cut down where he stood.

Viscount Curfew removed a silk handkerchief from his pocket and wiped the blood from Shably's sword before returning it to its scabbard.

'Mr Shably,' he said, in a very matter-of-fact tone.

The senior guard stood still, silently mesmerised by the sight at his feet.

'MR Shably,' Curfew repeated.

Eventually, Shably managed to turn his head.

'M-my lord?' he enquired, swallowing his fear and fighting back the urge to grit his teeth.

'This man was an evil, parasitic traitor. However, you may tell his family that he died in the course of his duty.'

'Y-yes, my lord.'

'And Shably?'

The senior guard met his master's stare.

'Lord Curfew?'

'From now on, I want that tunnel left unguarded until we are able to brick it up. That means no guards here and no guards inside; make sure you pass the order on to your seniors.'

'Sir.'

His words still echoing on the wind, the viscount turned and swept out of the garden.

For a time, nobody moved. The three guards looked at one another, but it seemed that none of them could muster the courage to speak.

Finally, after what seemed like an age, Shably knelt beside his fallen workmate and gently folded the man's arms over his chest.

'Stanhope was no traitor,' he whispered.

'Y-you probably shouldn't talk like that, Shably,' the ageing sentry intoned. 'It's not right to go against the word of the lor-'

'He's cracked!' Shably spat. 'Those kidnappers must've done something to him...either that, or I'm right in thinking-'

'Now hang on-' the wall-guard interrupted.

'No *you* hang on,' Shably continued. 'What's it been now, six months since they brought him back? Right! And how many have been killed for no reason? Three cooks, an assistant secretary and now a guard, too? How many of us can he murder before somebody sets him straight...'

'It'll be a good long time before anybody tries to put Lord Curfew straight, Shably...'

The ageing guard knelt next to his friend. 'I mean, who's going to have the guts to say anything: you?'

Shably sniffed, shook his head.

'Not me,' he said, despondently.

'Exactly! So we have to struggle through, as always...'

'Yeah...as always.'

'Did you see his face?' the wall-guard interrupted.

'What?' Shably looked up suddenly, his brow furrowed. 'Whose face?'

'Curfew's; it's all sagging on one side. I reckon he's ill.'

'Maybe,' said the old guard, smiling. 'We can only hope.'

CHAPTER
TWO

'Well, that was a lucky escape, wasn't it?'

Gape staggered along, wiping sweat from his brow with a silver handkerchief. 'I mean, it's a miracle we all came out with our lives really, isn't it GROAN?'

'Me? What did I do?'

Gordo removed his helmet and shoved it under one arm.

'You? Let's see now...hmm...YOU TOOK THE DAMN HAMMER WITHOUT WAITING TO SEE IF THE PLACE WAS BOOBY-TRAPPED; THAT'S WHAT YOU DID.'

The big barbarian shrugged.

'So what? We got out, di'nt we?'

'Yeah, by the skin of our teeth!' Gape exclaimed. 'I actually lost some skin in that door-snapper at the cave mouth!'

'Oh, stop moanin'. Anyone'd fink you never saw a trap before. Besides, we got the 'ammer, di'nt we?'

The trio walked on in silence for a while, before Gordo noticed something.

'Thick wood up ahead,' he announced. 'And there's an old building to the right, see?'

'It's an inn,' said Gape, without looking up. 'You always find them right in the middle of nowhere, especially up this way.'

'Shall we pop inside and have an ale?' Gordo asked the others. 'I could certainly do with one.'

'You and me both,' Gape agreed, and the three companions quickened their pace through the wood.

'Damn it!' Gape said, after a time, stopping dead in his tracks. 'Of all the black luck...'

Gordo frowned.

'What's the problem now?'

'It's abandoned.'

'How can you tell?'

'Hmm...I don't know. Maybe it's because all the windows are broken, or it might be because the door's hanging off. Take your pick.'

The mercenaries arrived at the building and Groan stepped inside, under a broken sign that said 'Lostings'.

'It ain't fallin' down,' he confirmed. 'Just a lot o' mess everywhere. 'Ere, maybe the taps're still workin'.'

'Yes,' said Gape. 'Let's see, shall we?' He marched across the reed-strewn floor and leaped over the bar in one swift movement.

'No,' he said, testing the ale taps. 'These barrels are empty.'

'Shame,' said Gordo. 'I'm going to have a quick look out the back. Anyone up for coming with me?'

'Nah,' said Groan, moodily. ''M tired, I am. I'm gonna rest up f'ra bit.'

'Me too,' said Gape, wearily. 'We could probably lie on these benches.

The two barbarians took their positions on the long benches while Gordo disappeared into the bowels of the building.

Time passed.

'Nobody here,' said Gordo, when he eventually returned from the back of the inn. 'There's a basement though; it's got a dungeon in it.'

'A dungeon?' said Gape, opening one eye. 'That's fairly unusual for an inn, isn't it?'

'Maybe it's a do-you-in,' said Groan, and followed the joke up with a laugh that sounded like a horse drowning.

'So, what are we doing?' Gordo continued.

Gape closed his open eye. 'Well,' he said, sleepily. 'I vote we rest up here for an hour and then head through the woods.'

The dwarf nodded.

'Good idea. If they're the Beanstalk Woods, and I think they are, we'll come out near Chudderford. Plus, if there's anything nasty in the woods, by resting up we'll be ready to deal with it.'

'Agreed.'

'Good,' said Gordo, finding his own bench to lie on. 'I found a mouse in the basement, too: looked as if it was on its last legs. That's the only sign of life in the entire place, though. I reckon goblins cleared out all the loot, if there ever was any. I don't think we should hang on here, either. I've got a really, really bad feeling about this place.'

'Do-you-in,' Groan muttered, still in stitches over the brilliance of his own wit.

'Ouch! Argh! Blimey: do these woods have anything living in them that doesn't eat you?' Groan and Gape Teethgrit immediately halted their progress to glance back at the dwarf, who was slapping himself all over.

'Why don't you stop complaining!' Gape snapped. 'After all, as Groan said, we just escaped a collapsing mountain and came out with the prize intact. You should be happy! We found your stupid hammer, didn't we?'

'It's not my hammer, Gape. It's a piece of Illmoor legend that's going to make Phlegm the richest kingdom on the continent.'

Gape frowned.

'Phlegm already is the richest kingdom on the continent' he said.

'It was,' Gordo said, darting a pointed glance at Groan. 'Until somebody drained all the coffers.'

'You're joking!' Gape exclaimed, clapping a hand over his mouth. 'But we can't have spent that much: there was an entire HALL full of gold when Groan took the throne from King Phew!'

'Yeah,' said Groan. 'I never got rid o' that much.'

Gordo stomped up to the big barbarian and thrust a stubby finger at his knotted kneecap. 'Yes you did, Groan Teethgrit! You spent the lot! I went in there last month; do you know what I found? Three gold pieces and a bacon sandwich! An entire fortune frittered away on wine, women, golden swords, ruby axes, women, lavish food, emerald crossbows, presents for women, and that ruddy diamond-encrusted posing pouch you've got on!'

'Snot like we didn' 'ave fun, tho,' Groan boomed. ''Ere, you 'member that big axe with the-'

'GROAN TEETHGRIT!' Gordo yelled, swinging his axe and burying it in a nearby tree. 'Don't you realise what you've done? You've put your crown, your brand new onyx-set, solid platinum crown in jeopardy for the sake of a few merry nights and a load of only-for-the-mantelpiece weaponry!'

'Yeah,' Groan agreed. 'Good, innit?'

'Oh, I give up!'

Gordo left his axe embedded in the tree and slumped onto a nearby stump.

'Where are we anyway?' Gape prompted, peering around at the darkening woods.

'I told you: Beanstalk Woods,' Gordo said, without looking up. 'Due west of Spittle, and north of Phlegm. There should be an old ruin somewhere along this path: we'll rest there and then start for home first thing tomorrow morning. That way, we can have a few days' relaxation before we have to go to Dullitch to flog the hammer on to Curfew.'

'Beanstalk Woods,' said Gape slowly, his brow furrowed. 'The name rings a bell, but I can't remember why...'

'I reckon Curfew 'll buy the hammer, don't you?' Gordo asked Groan, deliberately ignoring the other barbarian.

Groan frowned. 'If he don't, I'll punch 'im in the face.'

'Nice,' Gordo muttered. 'That'll be good for inter-city relations.'

'Beanstalk Wood!' Gape suddenly exclaimed. 'Isn't that where all the giant spiders are supposed to be?'

Gordo shook his head. 'Nah, that's Grinswood.

'I'm sure it's Beanstalk Woods,' Gape argued. 'Home of

the ancient spider-race of Inge, and their legendary King: Arachitrow: half man, half giant-spider.'

Gordo peered up at Gape and made a face. 'Where do you get all this stuff from?' he asked.

'I read the news-scrolls.'

'Oh: which one? *The Daily Drivel* or *The Weekly Rot?*'

'Ain't no such fing as a stinkin' spidey-king,' Groan boomed. 'If there 'ad a bin, I'd a bin up 'ere an' killed 'im.'

'Well you didn't,' said Gape, conclusively. 'Because he's standing right behind you.'

CHAPTER
THREE

The room was wreathed in shadow.

There were four candles on the table, each strategically positioned to form a perfect square around the centrepiece: a large crystal ball supported on the shoulders of four tiny lead wizards.

Viscount Curfew listened carefully until he heard the footfall of his personal guards echoing away, then he took a seat before the table, placed both hands flat on the oak surface, and concentrated.

'Dark Master of Lords Long Dead,' he muttered, closing his eyes and channelling all of his concentration into the ball. 'I call on you once again in order to give you a report of my progress...and to beg your assistance in sustaining my deception. You have already given me powers that mortal men could only dream of...now I have to ask for more.'

The ball shimmered, and then a form appeared inside it; a form so twisted and hideous that Curfew found it difficult to maintain his focus. It muttered a sentence of words that appeared to contain only an assortment of syllables. The language, which would have been alien to anyone not extremely well versed in the dark arts, was immediately understood.

'Yes, Dark Master,' Curfew replied. 'I kidnapped the viscount as you suggested, but the plan was foiled by meddlers from the city...and I had to advance stage two of the plan: therefore, Curfew is dead and I have taken his place on the throne of Dullitch. His body...is well hidden beneath magical territory. I...have put your *other* eye on it, Master. No-one will ever find-'

The form in the orb spoke again, each poisonous intonation dripping with malice.

'Yes,' answered the royal impostor. 'Everything proceeds according to your designs. I've been inside the palace for some time now and I should tell you that I *have*...seen the engraving you spoke of. You were right, Dark Master; it *does* have a place for the key.'

The creature in the orb muttered something, its vein-riddled lips parting to reveal teeth that were nothing more than blackened shards.

The impostor nodded.

'Yes...but, as you said, there is no way to force the main seal without it. Are you...still certain that the prophecy will come to pass?'

This time, the mutterings were almost spat out.

'No, Master! Of course I do not question your wisdom! What I meant to ask is if you were still certain that the key will find its way to the palace...but I see that you *are*, and again I marvel at your power. However, Dark Master, I need to buy more time in this disguise you have given me...if I am discovered in my true form, they will not hesitate to cast me dow-'

The words spoken next were uttered with such spite that each syllable felt like a thrown dagger, even to the shadowy wretch they addressed.

'I hear and obey, Master. And I have taken the city in accordance with your wishes,' said the impostor, now gesturing towards his sagging features. 'Yet...I am beginning to shed.'

There was a slight pause, then a bolt of light darted from the ball and surged into the impostor's face. He flew backwards, over the chair, screaming in agony and clutching his head as he crashed to the floor.

'Ahhhhhhh! The pain...it's worse!'

Again, the voice in the crystal spoke but, again, the words were maliciously spat out.

'Pllllllease stop it! Stop the p-'

The impostor's voice was suddenly silenced, as he lost all consciousness, and his mind vanished into the world of sleep.

DULLITCH COUNCIL's three most important officers bustled into the small room and took their seats opposite the man in the brightly-coloured suit. Burnie, the Troglodotion leader of the group, did a brilliant job of ignoring the funny hat and the pointy wisp of beard that had been dyed pink, and opted to look his guest directly in the eye instead. His colleagues tried the same tactic but were not so skilfully focussed as their superior.

'Effigy Spatula,' said Rin Lye, the council's senior judge, examining a scrap of parchment she'd unfurled. 'You are brought here before us on no less than twenty-seven counts of city vandalism, four counts of treason and, let me see, one threat of unattempted murder.'

'Unattempted murder?' Burnie enquired, leaning over to see if he could read the parchment himself.

'Yes, sir,' Rin Lye confirmed. 'He repeatedly threatened not to kill his neighbour's wife.'

'Is that an actual offence?' asked Taciturn Cadrick, vice chairman of the city council.

'Not as such,' the judge agreed. 'But as the saying goes: a threat made is a threat made.'

'Well, Mr. Spatula,' said Burnie, turning to the accused and shaking his waxy head. 'You are known to be one of the most inventive criminal minds in Illmoor. You also appear to have a great many questionable associates from all over Illmoor who seem only to expand your circle of mischief. I personally don't see why we should let you go free, but unfortunately these things aren't entirely my decision. What, um, *exactly* do you have to say for yourself, Mr Spatula?'

The man in the bright-coloured suit didn't move: he just continued to stare balefully out of the window.

'Mr Spatula?' Rin Lye added, her voice betraying a hint of annoyance.

'EFFIGY SPATULA!' Burnie boomed.

The accused man suddenly turned his attention from the window, shuffled his chair into place and removed cotton balls from both ears.

'I'm so sorry,' he said. 'Were you talking to me?'

Burnie frowned a little and glanced at both of his colleagues before he spoke again.

'You *are* Effigy Spatula?' he hazarded. 'Formerly of thirty-seven Stainer Street?'

Effigy nodded.

'I am indeed,' he said, politely. 'And what can I do for you?'

Rin Lye muttered something under her breath. Then, seeing that everyone else was still in a state of mild amusement, she proceeded: 'This is your *hearing*, Mr Spatula. You understand that, don't you?'

'Oh yes,' said Effigy, nodding. 'It's perfectly understandable. By "perfectly understandable" I *mean* that, in your eyes, I've done some truly terrible things and I really should be punished.'

Taciturn Cadrick leaned forward in his chair.

'You *have* been punished, Mr Spatula. You've just spent six months in prison!'

Effigy fiddled with his sleeves.

'Mmm, well, of course I know *this* to be true,' he muttered. 'But I didn't learn anything from my stay in the dungeons; and I fully intend to go right out there and do the whole lot again: lock stock, in fact.'

'I beg your pardon?' Rin Lye exclaimed, raising herself slightly in her chair. 'Are you suggesting-'

'I'm not suggesting anything,' Effigy corrected her. 'I'm *telling* you that if you let me out, I'll immediately start causing the *same* trouble again. It *really* is the only thing that makes any difference in this place...'

'How dare you!' Rin Lye screamed, thrusting an accusatory finger at him. 'I'll see you *hanged* for this insolence. I'll have you s-'

'Mr Spatula,' Burnie interrupted, giving him an appraising glance. He took the parchment from the irate judge and stared hard at the scrawl that adorned it. 'Why do you do this, exactly?'

'Mmm?' Effigy mumbled. 'You mean why do I choose to fight for the things I believe in? Because I can.'

Burnie ushered the outraged councillors into silence with one wave of his glutinous finger.

'OK, then. Well, just out of interest, what do you believe in, Mr Spatula?'

Effigy suddenly cracked a smile.

'I believe in freedom, little troglodyte. This city was founded by *normal men* and those *normal* men have a right to govern it. We don't want or need this endless line of inbred dukes, barons and viscounts to run it.'

'If I may, Mr Spatula,' said Burnie, carefully. 'This city was founded by *thieves*...and no one in their right mind would want them in charge again. We've spent the best part of the Tri-age attempting to undo the damage *they* caused... and, incidentally, my name is Burnie.'

Effigy nodded.

'Then that is your opinion, Burnie, and you're very entitled to it...because you're a FREE speaker. And so am I.'

'No, Mr Spatula,' Taciturn interrupted. 'You're an arsonist, a thief, a vandal and an agitator. You're also a menace to society.'

Effigy smiled broadly.

'Thank you very much,' he said. 'That means a lot coming from a man of letters.'

Burnie folded his arms and leaned back in his chair.

'You may leave us now, Mr Spatula, but I'll give you the following warning: if you are ever brought before us again, you will face the noose. Is that clear?'

'Crystal.' Effigy jumped to his feet. 'Can you actually see through crystal, I wonder?'

'Don't push it,' Taciturn muttered, rising from his chair and opening the door for the man.

Effigy bowed low and departed.

'He *has* to be stopped,' said Rin Lye, slamming her fist on the tabletop.

'I agree,' added Taciturn, quickly. 'That man is an example of everything that's wrong with this city.'

Burnie nodded and rose from his own chair.

'I think I'll give him one last warning,' he said, rushing to the door. 'You know, just to make certain that he understands.'

Effigy had reached the end of the corridor and was about to descend the first flight of steps to the ground floor of City Hall when the troglodyte caught him up.

'One more thing, Mr Spatula!' Burnie called, waddling up to the freedom fighter.

Effigy turned on his heel and grinned his flash, expansive grin.

'Yes, your honour?' Burnie grabbed the man's arm and pulled him close.

'Midnight: Rotting Ferret,' he whispered. 'And don't tell anyone where you're going, or I'll kill you myself.'

CHAPTER
FOUR

The battle in the forest was getting into its stride. Gape Teethgrit, who didn't like spiders in the normal way, was rooted to the spot with fear. All around him, blades flashed, sending long spindly black legs whirling into the air. He decided there and then that *up* was probably the best choice of direction.

Gordo Goldaxe was moving remarkably fast for a dwarf. Having hacked limbs from more than a dozen of the eight-legged warriors, he was now resorting to an axe-of-death manoeuvre that did nothing for his muscles but made him practically impossible to bite.

Groan, on the other hand, was facing up to the Spider King. The creature, which looked the same as the rest of its race apart from an all-too-human face, began to rise on its many legs and scream in an arcane language.

'Havit. Friyaes; Innkwou!'

'What d-did it say?' Gape enquired, having climbed halfway up a nearby tree.

'Dunno,' Groan admitted, readying his sword and driving it towards the beast. 'Who cares?'

'It probably wasn't "Welcome to my lair",' Gordo hazarded, finishing the axe-spin and pausing to catch his breath. 'Maybe "Havit" is spider for "get out of here"?'

''Avit yourself!' Groan yelled, bombing into the Spider King and hacking manically at its stomach. 'Avit! Avit! Avit!'

The creature retreated several steps to avoid the blows, then charged forwards again and spewed a sickly green liquid over the immediate area. Sensing their monarch's action, the remaining spiders all did the same, spraying out enough emerald gunk to fill the entire clearing.

Groan dropped his sword and quickly snatched at his face, squeezing the horrid mixture from his eyes and spitting mouthfuls of it onto the grass.

Gordo had been captured; six spiders were taking it in turns to spin a thick-stranded web around him. The more the little dwarf struggled, the more entangled he became in the web.

'Help me, Groan! Help meeee!'

'I can't see!' the barbarian roared. 'I got all this weird stuff in me face and it feels like it's burnin' me skin off.'

'It probably is! Arggh! They've got my leg, now!'

'Where's me sword? I can't find me sword!'

'GAPE!' Gordo screamed. 'HELP US!'

The long-haired barbarian looked down from his hiding place in the tree, released a long sigh and counted to ten. Then he dropped from the branch and twirled both his blades as if they were yo-yo's

'It's always *me me me* with you two!' he screamed, flying around the clearing like a man possessed and hacking apart every spider he came into contact with. 'No matter that *I* might have a *phobia*, no matter that *I* might be deathly afraid of spiders. Oh no, *that* would be *too selfish* of me, wouldn't it?'

He danced away from a spun web, sidestepped two liquid sprays and hacked open Gordo's sticky prison, causing the little dwarf to roll out and crawl around the clearing in search of his battleaxe.

'I don't know,' Gape continued, throwing one of his swords right through a spider and spearing it to a tree. 'I'm getting fed up with you two, I really, truly am.' He came to a standstill beside Groan's sword, swept it from the ground and threw it to his brother, who'd at last recovered from his temporary blindness.

'Now,' Gape said, removing his own blade from the creature skewered against the tree. 'Are you going to kill this Spider King or not?'

'Yeah,' said Groan, purposefully.

'Good. So I can go back into the tree and hide, can I?'

''F ya want.'

'Yes, I do. Thank you very much indeed.'

Gape quickly ran back to his tree and began to shin up the trunk.

Meanwhile, Gordo had made short work of several of the remaining spiders; reducing them to a pile of bulbous abdomens and spindly limbs in his furious embarrassment at being imprisoned. The few remaining spiders stayed at a safe distance, none too keen to continue the attack.

Groan marched squarely up to the Spider King.

'Give up,' he boomed, 'an' I won't kill ya...much.'

The giant king darted forward, a look of alien glee on his tiny face. His eight legs took him across the clearing in seconds, but Groan wasn't there. Sensing the sudden departure of its prey, the great spider, swiftly shuffled around...and its head was sliced cleanly from its body.

'I told 'im ta give up.'

The creature immediately collapsed in an untidy heap at Groan's feet, and the giant barbarian drove his blade into the ground.

Sensing the fall of their leader, the last few spiders slowly shrank away from the party and withdrew into the depths of the forest.

A dark and uneasy silence fell over the clearing.

'Is it OK to come down now?' Gape asked.

Gordo peered up into the tree. 'I'm shocked,' he said. 'I've never seen you fight so well...'

'And you never will again,' said the warrior, swinging down from the tree and landing on his feet. 'As I've said before, on more than one occasion, I'm utterly sick to the back teeth of you; the pair of you. When we get to Dullitch, I'm quitting this trio.' He smiled faintly and began to wander off down the path.

'Some king he was,' Groan boomed, wrenching his sword free and pointing at the giant spider. 'He din't get me once, 'f ya don't count all tha' sick.'

'Not once?' Gordo repeated, his eyebrows shifting in surprise. He gave Groan an appraising glance. 'Maybe old age is making you tougher.'

'I ain't old,' said the giant barbarian. 'I'm jus' gone furty-'

'...seven,' Gordo finished.

'Eh?'

'You're just gone thirty-seven, Groan.'

''Ang on-'

'Hang on for what? You're a year younger than me and I'm thirty-eight, remember?'

Groan's eyebrows knitted.

'What happened to furty-last?'

'Thirty-Last? You don't mean thirty-nine?'

'Yeah.'

'That's next year.'

Groan muttered something under his breath.

'What was that?'

'I said, I don' 'stand why folk keep movin' the ages.'

'People DON'T move the ages,' Gordo said, rolling his eyes. 'It's YOU that does that: age always works the same way. You start off young and then you get old.'

'No' always,' Groan protested. 'Grandma Teethgrit go' younger 'vry year.'

'No she didn't!' screamed the dwarf. 'She probably told you that to stop you from finding out her real age.'

'Nah, you're 'rong,' said Groan, shaking his head. 'She died young; she was only furty when they buried 'er...'

'Oh, wake up, will you?' Gordo snapped. 'She had skin like a saddlebag and a face like brown paper left three days in the rain!'

'So?'

'So she was more like a hundred and ten!'

'Excuse me,' said Gape, patiently. 'I'm sorry to interrupt such a vital conversation about a past member of our family, but I've found something you might both be quite interested to see...'

RORGRIM RIPPLE, the new owner of the Rotting Ferret Inn, was just reaching up to slide over the top bolt when someone knocked at the door.

'We're closed,' Rorgrim shouted, moving on to the next bolt. 'Come back in the morn-.'

'I'm here to see Burnie,' said the voice outside. 'He told me to come at midnight.'

Rorgrim sighed, rolled his eyes and began to undo the bolts.

'Hold on a minute, I'll let you in.'

The door was pulled open to reveal the lanky form of Effigy Spatula, who strode into the inn, removed his hat and took a low, theatrical bow. He was quite disappointed when he looked up again to see that his audience had turned away from him. Still, he forced a grin:

'My name, good man, is-'

'I'm not interested.'

'What?'

'I'm not interested in your name.' Rorgrim finished at the door and began to wander across to the tables. 'Meeting's downstairs, and the troglodyte doesn't like to be kept waiting.'

'I see.' Effigy bit his lip and twisted his hat in his hands. 'Like that, is it?'

'It is.'

'Well, then...I'd better run.'

'You better had.'

Rorgrim watched the young man leap the bar in a single movement and disappear behind the curtain. Then he stared dispassionately at his grimy fingernails and began to scrub the tables.

Effigy descended two flights of stairs and proceeded along a short passage that terminated at a little wooden door. He didn't bother to knock.

'Good evening, gentlemen,' he announced, flinging the

door wide and bowing, once again, with grace. 'I am Effigy Spatula, Freedom Fighter and Man of the Age. And you are?'

He looked up at a room full of lanterns, and two very unimpressed faces. One of them belonged to Burnie, the troglodotion council chairman, and the other, unmistakably, was that of an ogre.

Burnie sighed.

'Sit down please, Mr Spatula.'

'I'm – what is – sorry?'

'I said: sit down.'

Effigy frowned. 'What exactly do you-'

'SIT DOWN OR I'LL RIP YOUR LEGS OFF,' the ogre cut in, pulling a heavy club from beneath the table and slamming it onto the floor.

Effigy practically dived into the seat.

'Good man. Now, my name is Burnie-'

'I know.'

'- and this here is Nazz, the ogre. Together, we make up the Royal Society of Lantern Collectors. I've brought you here tonight to have a look at some of our rarest pieces...'

Burnie wriggled down from his chair, waded through the clutter and ended up in the dark recesses of the room. He returned with an ordinary-looking lantern.

'This,' he said to his highly confused guest, 'is the Musterlight Three, takes seven candles and has an original sliding door-piece. Nazz?'

The ogre clambered to his feet and peered around before snatching up a wide but equally unremarkable-looking lantern.

'The Foggstriker Four,' he announced. 'Known for its sliding tray and two candle-capacity.'

Effigy boggled at both creatures, but he was still very

conscious of the ogre's club.

'And, last but not least,' Burnie continued, locating yet another rusty old piece, 'the Shadowstalker Twelve, famous for its tinted casing and engraved handle.' He put down the latest relic and turned to his guest, with a warm smile. 'Any questions?'

Effigy frowned, then coughed a few times, folded his arms and frowned again.

'I'm sorry?' he said, tentatively, looking from Burnie to Nazz and back again.

'Do you have any questions?' Burnie repeated, his rubbery lips glistening in the half-light of the room.

'Y-yes, actually I-'

'Go ahead. ASK THEM.'

'Well-' Effigy peered hopefully at the ogre. 'If I do, will I get my arms broken?'

'Not if you ask the right ones.'

'OK.' Effigy nodded, nervously. 'What exactly am I doing here?'

Burnie shrugged.

'You're looking at lanterns.'

'OK, fine, but what I mean is, why did *you* ask me here?'

'To look at lanterns.'

'Ah; I think I'm getting it,' said Effigy, stroking his jet wisp of beard. 'In that case, what are *you* doing here?'

'We're showing you the lanterns.'

'Agreed. But why?'

'Because we're the Royal Society of Lantern Collectors.'

'Are you really?'

Burnie suddenly smiled and leaned forward, grasping Effigy by his collar. 'Not really. NO.'

'Ah...so who are you really?'

Nazz the ogre gave a toothy grin.

'That was the right question,' he boomed, and slapped Effigy so hard on the back that his spine cracked.

'Exactly the right question,' Burnie echoed, reaching up and tugging on Effigy's arm. 'Follow me to the brass lantern on the far wall and I'll endeavour to explain...'

CHAPTER
FIVE

'I tripped on a tree root,' Gape explained, forcing his way through the undergrowth. 'And I knew I was going to fall, so I reached up to save myself, pulled on this branch and, suddenly, the whole clearing starts to mutate and, then it appears from nowhere...'

'What are you talking about?'

Groan and Gordo followed Gape into a strange clearing in the wood, where the winding weeds of the forest were evidently trying to overcome a small and ancient-looking stone chapel.

'This place just appeared?' said Gordo, treading carefully through the grass.

'It's quite safe,' Gape assured him. 'If there were pit traps in grass this low, they'd be covered with bracken.'

'Yeah,' said Gordo. 'I'll keep walking like this if it's all the same to you.' He wasn't taking any chances; he'd fought some forest-dwelling clerics in his time, and all of them set devilish traps around their churches.

'D'ya reckon' there's 'ny loot in there?' Groan boomed,

stamping across the grass like an angry giant. 'I'll 'ave the door down so we can see.'

'Wait!' Gordo yelled. 'Stay where you are! We don't know *what's* inside that place! There could be a griffin or a ruddy purple dragon, for crying out loud; you can't just charge into these places!'

Groan frowned. 'Why not?'

The dwarf rolled his eyes.

'Just because! I mean, what happens in the admittedly unlikely event that there's something inside that you can't handle?'

'Yeah? Like what?'

'Like, like...like a froglord!'

'I killed one o' them.'

'A troll?'

'I done six moon trolls an' a rock troll in one fight...'

Gordo thought for a moment.

'What about...a Demon King?'

'A Demon King 'd kill me,' said Groan.

'Right! Exactly! And what happens after that?'

'Dunno: I s'pose it'd kill you, 'an all.

'And then what have we gained?'

'Eh?'

Gordo folded his arms. 'What would we have gained from charging in if we're all slaughtered by a Demon King?'

'Hang on a minute,' said Gape, attempting to flash his least insulting smile. 'Using your own argument, surely if there's a Demon King inside this chapel, it's not going to matter whether we rush the place or knock on the door and wait for an invite: the damn thing'll kill us either way. It's not going to say "Oh, all right then, I'll let the bald one off because he rang the bell."'

'Agreed, but anyway, there's NOT a Demon King inside...'

'There isn't?' Gape exclaimed, sardonically. 'How do you know?'

'Of course there isn't!' screamed Gordo, slamming his axe into the ground. 'I made it up as a point of argument: There's no such thing as a Demon King!'

'Says you! There's probably two of them in there-'

A sudden eruption of sound caused the pair to stop mid-squabble. Groan had kicked down the door.

'No demons,' he confirmed. 'Stinks, though.'

Gape hurried over to the entrance and peered around his brother: light had streamed into the little building.

'There're a few rats,' Gape noted.

'Rats,' repeated Gordo, sniffing the air suspiciously. 'Dangerous, rats are.'

Gape shook his head.

'Not this lot; they look grateful for the company.'

''Ere,' Groan said, stepping over a short and crusty pew that had toppled just inside the arch. 'I reckon this place is one o' them really old an' 'bandoned sorts.'

'It's old,' Gordo agreed, 'but it certainly isn't abandoned.'

Gape glanced down at him.

'Why do you say that, o' short one?'

'Well, for a start, the lock's been replaced, and recently: there's a clear outline around it and the brass is still shining.'

'There's something I don't like here,' Gape announced, stalking between the remaining pews with an inquisitive look on his face. 'Something I don't like at all.'

'I'm with you,' said Gordo, uneasily. 'Look at the floor: mountains of dust and footprints running right the way through!'

'Footprints?' Gape enquired, squinting at the floor.

'City boots,' said Groan quickly. 'I know; I can tell 'em anywhere: fournailers.'

Gordo frowned.

'Fournaliars; what does *that* mean?'

'It's a type of boot,' Gape hazarded, trying to remember his father's hellish tracking lessons. 'A good type, too: very expensive. It basically means the boots are from Dullitch.'

'I don't get it!' Gordo snapped. 'Dullitch is miles from here! Why would a well-off *Dullitch* citizen come down to a chapel in a wood in the middle of nowhere to replace a lock? It doesn't make any sense!' He squinted at the prints. 'Hmm, let's see where they lead...'

'You can see where they lead from here,' Gape muttered, pointing towards the stone altar at the far end of the chapel. 'This place isn't exactly *big*.'

Groan stomped up the centre aisle and crouched down beside the altar.

'Footsteps stop 'ere,' he said.

Gordo nodded. 'Do they go around the back?'

'Nah.'

'You know what that means?' Gape called.

'Yeah,' said Groan. 'Means I get to do this.'

Groan dropped to his knees, put one shoulder to the altar stone and heaved at it. There was a loud grinding noise and the stone began to move aside.

'Staircase underneath?' Gordo hazarded, knowing the answer before Gape could run up and check.

'Yes! It's only wide enough to go one abreast, though. Are we all going?'

'I am,' said Groan. 'There might be gold 'n' stuff down there.'

'That counts me in,' Gordo added. 'I don't miss opportunities with the word gold in them.'

'Well, I'm going whether you like it or not,' Gape snapped. 'There's no way I'm playing lookout twice in one day.'

'Fair enough.'

'Yeah.' Gape stuck out his jaw. 'Shall I go first?'

'Nah,' Groan boomed. 'I always go first.'

'Why is that again?'

''Cos I'm the 'ardest.'

'Really? And what brings you to that conclusion, dear brother of mine?'

'Oh, don't start all that rubbish!' Gordo screamed, elbowing past Gape's knotted left knee. 'Just get down the stairs, will you? If we hang about here much longer, that Demon King will probably turn up...'

'I don't know if anyone's interested,' Gape muttered. 'But I found us a useful tor-'

'Shh!' Gordo put a finger to his lips. 'We need to be quiet, here-'

'But-'

'Shut up!'

Gape counted to ten under his breath and followed.

WHEN HE REACHED the far wall, Burnie gripped the mounted brass lantern and turned it through one hundred and eighty degrees. A section of masonry slid away...and Effigy Spatula gasped.

The large, circular table in the room beyond contained six chairs: three were occupied.

'Allow me to introduce you around, Mr Spatula,' said Burnie, taking one of the empty seats and motioning for Effigy to choose another. Nazz took the third.

'Working around from your left, we have Jimmy Quickstint, gravedigger and master thief-'

'Pleased to meet you.'

'-Brim Shably, a senior guard up at the palace-'

'Evening.'

'-Jareth Obegarde, a vampire detective-'

'Loftwing, actually: charmed, I'm sure.'

'...and, of course, you've met Nazz.'

Effigy nodded at the ogre.

'Yes, unfortunately I have.'

Burnie smiled in conclusion.

'Collectively, we make up the Secret Army of Dullitch.'

'And not, in fact, the Royal Society of Lantern Collectors?'

'No.'

Effigy smiled wanly, but the rest of his face contorted.

'I presume the landlord's in on this?' he asked. 'I mean, he's probably not going to allow you people to move his walls around without prior arrangement.'

'Correct. Rorgrim turns a blind eye to our little gatherings and, in exchange for a few gold a week, tells everybody we're the Royal Society of Lantern Collectors.'

'Yes,' said Effigy, grinning. 'A story given much substance by your false room, back there.'

Burnie scratched his rubbery nose. 'Spot on. I can see you're a keen observer, Mr Spatula.'

'Not really; I just see what people show me. Now, if you don't mind me asking, and if you're not collecting lanterns or something pointless like that, WHAT in fact are you doing, and why?'

Burnie smiled at the rest of the group, who all remained pensively silent.

'I'm glad you asked, Mr Spatula. Basically, we're rebels. We believe in all the same things as you: we think that the city should be a haven for Freedom, Hope, Justice and Peace.'

Effigy shook his head in disbelief.

'But you're in charge of the Dullitch Council! You can bring about those things yourself!'

'Ha! If only that were so, Mr Spatula, if only that were so. The council lost all its real power during the reign of Duke Modeset. After the rat catastrophe, Viscount Curfew ascended to the throne and took on most of the actual decision-making...'

'So you decided to create a social club instead?' Effigy smiled, but Burnie wasn't smiling with him.

'We're not a social club, Mr Spatula. We started as a secret support group for the viscount; a group set up to find and defeat Lord Curfew's enemies. These days, we're activists...and we want you to join us.'

'I see. Activists, eh? And what exactly is it that you are trying to activate?'

There were several nervous glances around the table before Burnie answered the question.

'I'll tell you, Mr Spatula: we're trying to have Viscount Curfew removed from the throne of Dullitch.'

'W-what? I thought you said you supported-'

'Our mission changed six months ago, when the viscount was rescued from his kidnappers and restored to the throne...'

Effigy frowned. 'I don't get it; you mean you all supported him until six months ago? That's a sudden turnaround, isn't it? What changed after he was kidnapped?'

There were several murmurs at the table.

'Only one thing changed,' said Burnie, leaning back in his chair. 'Unfortunately, it's a big thing. We're pretty sure that the man sitting on the throne of Dullitch right at this second *isn't* Viscount Curfew.'

'Very sure,' added Obegarde.

'Almost certain,' Burnie finished.

Effigy pursed his lips to let out a chuckle when he saw that nobody else around the table was smiling.

'You're not serious?' he hazarded. 'You're not actually, genuinely serious?'

'Deadly,' said Obegarde, his single elongated fang gleaming in the candlelight.

'He is,' added Jimmy Quickstint, tiredly. 'We all are.'

'I apologise, then,' said Effigy, trying to keep up with the scope of the conversation. 'But if you're actually expecting me to believe that it isn't Viscount Curfew on the Dullitch throne; then who in the name of gods do you think it is? I mean, whoever the chap is, he *looks* a lot like Curfew...and he certainly *acts* like him. That 'No Drinking In The Market Place' law he passed the other week was characteristically crackers!'

'The impostor is identical to Lord Curfew in every way,' confirmed Shably, the guard. 'An' he sounds like him, too. There's barely a difference between 'em.'

'A twin, then,' Effigy suggested, beginning to enjoy being part of the strange gathering. 'You hear of secret twins all the time, especially in royal circles. They're ten a penny.'

'Not twins,' said Nazz, sounding surprisingly lucid for an ogre. 'I was royal bodyguard the night Lord Curfew was born, and I can tell you that only one baby arrived.'

'What then? A magician of some sort? Or a creature with the same abilities – a shape shifter?'

'Possibly,' said Burnie, pointing over at Shably. 'Our friend at the palace says his face was sagging the other day, when he killed that guard.'

'Curfew killed a guard?' Effigy stroked his beard thoughtfully. 'Why would he do that?'

Shably swallowed, as if the very thought of what he was about to say made him nauseous. 'In my opinion, he killed Private Stanhope because he was stationed at the secret escape tunnel outside his private chamber. Maybe the boy saw something he shouldn't have seen: he certainly looked as if he'd seen something extraordinary. In addition, when I was on duty yesterday night, Curfew's face was sagging like a weighted sack, and I've never seen his lordship looking like that before.'

'Hmm...' Effigy began, drumming his fingers on the tabletop. 'Could you possibly draw me a plan of this tunnel...and where it comes out?'

'Of course; it's in the Summer Gardens. Here...'

As Shably found a spare piece of parchment and began to scrawl on it, Effigy turned back to the others.

'So who do we think Lord Curfew really is? And how long do we think he has not been...himself?'

'Since the kidnapping,' said Jimmy Quickstint.

'He was fine before that awful business,' Shably agreed, finishing his plan and passing it to Effigy, who stuffed the parchment into a breast pocket.

'Definitely the kidnap,' Obegarde agreed. 'I did hope we'd foiled it, but I'm beginning to think it was we who were foiled! Somewhere along the line, a switch was made and Curfew...well, we can only assume he was murdered. Enoch

Dwellings, a friend of mine who led the rescue attempt, is absolutely convinced I'm wrong and that Curfew *is* himself...but I think that's his pride talking: he can't bring himself to believe that it wasn't the viscount he rescued: hence his decision to take no involvement with the group...'

Effigy whistled between his teeth.

'Hmm...then, if you lot are to be believed, we could have a magically-charged, shape-switching murderer on the throne of our city.

There were a series of reluctant nods.

'Ha!' Effigy exclaimed. 'Even more of a reason to dethrone the lords and reach for our freedom.'

'Exactly, Mr Spatula,' said Burnie, noting several excited grins. 'And that's right where you come in.'

CHAPTER
SIX

A torch flared in the darkness.

'Where'd ya get that?' Groan boomed, when the flames practically removed his new chin-beard.

'I did *try* to tell you earlier, but you weren't listening.'

'Well, I'm listening now!'

Gape shrugged.

'I found it inside a hollow when I was hiding in the tree,' he confirmed, handing the torch down to his brother and then moving aside to let Gordo through. 'There's a message scrawled along the side in the old language; says it's enchanted and never goes out.'

'That'll be 'andy,' said Groan, snatching the torch and proceeding down the stone steps.

'What can you see?' Gordo whispered, following the giant barbarian down into the dark.

'Not much yet, jus' a load o' cobwebs an' stuff.'

'Well, tell me when you see something! I hate going down tunnels with you two; I never get to see anything!'

'Well, you don't need to worry about me,' said Gape, resentfully. 'I'd have a job to mess up the view standing *behind* you, wouldn't I?'

'Oh, I don't know – I'm sure you'd manage somehow...'

'Shhh! I can 'ear somefing.'

Gordo and Gape ceased their banter and tried to stay silent. There was a very low hum coming from somewhere below them.

'What is it?' the dwarf enquired, excitedly.

'Dunno. Sounds like an 'um.'

Gape nodded. 'Definitely sounds like magic of some sort; should we look for traps?'

'How're we supposed to do that?' said Gordo, rolling his eyes. 'I can't even see my damn knees!'

'Well, we could always send you down; if you come back full of arrows, we know it's dangerous.'

'Ha ha. Don't make me laugh. You and Groan'll be real sorry the day you lose me: I'm the brains of this outfit.'

Gape nodded in the dark.

'You're absolutely right. If *you* weren't around, it would leave a real hole in my life.'

'Yeah? Well, I hope you fall *in it*.'

'Shh!' Groan interrupted. 'There's a shrine down 'ear. I can see a coffin.'

Groan reached the base of the stairs, fitted the enchanted torch into a convenient wall sconce, and took a few careful steps into the room. The others quickly followed him, trying not to step on each other's heels.

The chamber beyond was small and quite bare, and it did contain a plain-looking wooden coffin, but there was something altogether more alarming about it...

'It's been swept,' Gape observed, pointing at a broom

propped against the near wall. 'And the plaque on the coffin's been polished.'

'There's a plaque?' Gordo exclaimed. 'What's it say? Oh please let it be a king! They *always* bury them with their crown on.'

'It's not going to be a king,' said Gape, dismissively. 'I mean, look at this place, a tiny chapel in the middle of a thick wood with no life around for miles...'

'A magically-concealed chapel that you only found by accident,' Gordo corrected him. 'A magically concealed chapel, I might add, in a forest guarded by an army of giant spiders.'

'Yes, yes, all right! But you're wrong about there being nothing around for miles: what about the inn?'

'What; the Lostings place? That was an abandoned wreck; even the goblins had been at it!'

'There was still 'life' in it.'

'You mean that asthmatic mouse I found in the basement? That died while we were there!'

'So? There's still life around here; loads if you count the spide-.'

'Shut up! Groan's going for the coffin.'

All eyes turned as the big barbarian edged his way towards the shrine, putting each booted foot tentatively forward to test the stones for traps. Fortunately, the floor appeared to be genuine.

Groan leaned over the coffin.

'What does it say?' Gordo asked again. 'King what?'

'I dunno,' admitted Groan. 'I don' read, do I?' And with that, he jammed his sword into the coffin and wrenched off the lid. A purple glow filled the room; with it came a warm and slightly fetid stench.

''Sa dead body,' Groan observed. ''S glowin' an' all. Can't see if there's anyfing else yet...'

Gape covered his mouth as Groan reached into the coffin and started to rummage around.

Gordo, meanwhile, hurried over to the discarded lid and dragged it under the torchlight.

'Cayoeadit?' said Gape.

'Take your hand away from your mouth: I can't understand what you're saying.'

'Sorry. Can you read it?'

'Not unless I can turn – hang on – that's caught it. Now I can see the plaque...it says 'Sorrell Diveal, Highborn Lord of Illmoor.'

'Highborn Lord? Hmm...I don't recognise the name. He didn't govern a city, did he?'

'You've never heard of the Highborn?'

'Nope. Should I have?'

Gordo rolled his eyes.

'Don't you know anything, Gape Teethgrit? You're worse than your brother! The Highborn Lords of Illmoor were descended from the original rulers. There were eight of them: Muttknuckles-'

'-Baron of Sneeze,' Gape pointed out, to show he did know *some* things.

'-Blood-'

'-Prince of Legrash.'

'-Ozryk-'

'-Earl of Beanstalk.'

'WAS the Earl of Beanstalk: he's long dead, that one. Now you've interrupted me; where was I?'

'You'd done three.'

'Right. So Muttknucles, Blood and Ozryk, who died. Then

there's Lord Curfew of Dullitch, Visceral of Spittle and Duke Modeset, who we all knew only too well.'

Gape frowned in the torchlight.

'That's still only six.'

'Right,' Gordo agreed. 'But I've not mentioned the other two yet because they really were a breed apart. First, there was Vadney Sapp; he went bad when they didn't give him *some* throne or other; trained himself up to be a necromancer and – word has it – disappeared from Illmoor when a spell he'd done to summon a black dragon backfired and sent him through a vortex.'

'Wow,' Gape grinned. 'That's some knowledge you've got there, short stuff.'

'Well, when you're a mercenary, you pick these things up: local legends, you know.'

'Right. I'm assuming the last one was Sorrell Diveal?'

Gordo nodded. 'He was another bad sort, trained as a sorcerer in Shinbone, then went nuts and tried to destroy the entire town by raining fireballs on the place. The townsfolk tried to fight back for a time, but he was too strong. Then reinforcements arrived from Crust and they managed to turn the tide against him. He vanished.'

'Aha! Only now we know where he went, right?'

'Yeah, not that there's much of him to see, judging by the smell. Eh, Groan?'

'Nah, matter o' fac' he looks fresh. I don' see no gold, though. He's only got a chain fingy and a box in there wiv 'im.'

'Hang on,' said Gordo waddling over to the coffin. 'What do you mean, he looks fresh? He stinks to the high heavens!'

'Yeah, but he's still fresh. He can't have bin dead long.'

Gordo climbed up on the stone and peered into the coffin.

'That's odd,' he said, covering his mouth. 'The stink is unbelievable but the body looks as if it's just sleeping.'

'I'm in no hurry to see, either way,' said Gape. 'Is it definitely Diveal?'

'Not sure,' Gordo replied, squinting at the corpse. 'I think so: I've only ever seen one picture of him.'

'It is 'im,' Groan added. 'There was a big picture of 'im wiv them uvver lords in the Phlegm vault.'

'Was there?' said Gordo, surprised. 'I never saw it.'

'Nah, I swapped it wiv a merchant for a two-handed sword.'

'Ah, that'd explain it. Is the chain any good?'

'Yeah, looks 'eavy.'

'What about the box? Shall I lift it out?'

'Yeah: I'm not doin' it; s' prob'ly magic an' I 'ate magic.'

'Right.'

Gordo reached in and plucked out the box. Then he climbed down to the floor and placed the box squarely in the centre of the room.

'Right. You know the drill, boys: everyone draw.'

Gordo unhooked his battleaxe and put it on the floor beside the box while Groan drew a giant, double-handed sword and Gape quickly produced two longswords, which he twirled enthusiastically.

'Ready?'

'Ready.'

'Yeah, 'm ready.'

Gordo unclasped the box latch and flipped open the lid.

There was a crystal ball inside.

'YOU WANT ME TO WHAT?'

Effigy Spatula leaped up from the table, almost banging his head on a ceiling lantern that swung over it. 'Are you all insane?'

'I don't understand,' said Burnie, quietly. 'What's the problem? You hate the monarchy, don't you?'

'Well, yes, but-'

'And you want freedom and justice for all?'

'Of course, but listen-'

'And you told me you were going to go right out and commit a load of crimes anyway-'

'Yes, but not the sort of thing *you've* got in mind. I was going to start campaigning, do some minor vandalism, maybe knock over a few public statues: I wasn't going to murder anyone!'

Burnie folded his arms.

'We're not asking you to murder anyone, Mr Spatula. We're asking you, as a vocal freedom fighter and devoted campaigner for justice, to lead our secret group.'

'Yes,' Effigy acknowledged. 'But you've just told me that your secret group is planning to assassinate the bloody viscount!'

'He's NOT the viscount,' Shably argued. 'He's an evil impostor.'

'Well, whatever and *whoever* he is, you're asking me to kill him.'

'No, we're not!' Burnie snapped. 'We're asking you to help find a few good assassins who'll do the job for us! That's not murder, is it?'

'And if these yet-to-be-approached assassins fail to do the job?'

There were some carefully exchanged glances before Jimmy Quickstint spoke.

'There is a back-up plan,' he said.

'Oh good,' said Effigy. 'Let's hear that, shall we? It's got to be better than the original one.'

'Yes, it's pretty good,' Jimmy admitted. 'We both dress as guards, and I sneak you into the palace cellars.'

Effigy waited, but nothing else was said.

'And then what?' he prompted, noting Jimmy's blank expression.

'Then you set light to the fumeback powder that we'd have already planted down there and blow the place sky high.'

Effigy's mouth dropped open.

'What, you mean the palace? That's mass murder! There must be more than twenty staff in there, not counting the hundred or so guards!'

'No worries,' said Shably, with confidence. 'I'll make sure they're all out.'

'You're all crazy,' Effigy said, beginning to walk around the outside of the room. 'I mean, I understand why you believe the Curfew impostor thing, and why you want him gone, but the fact is that you don't even know for sure if it IS an impostor on the throne. Don't you think it might be an idea to find out one way or another *before* you plan the assassination attempts?'

'We could never find out for certain,' said Burnie, sadly. 'If Shably's with the viscount half of every day and most of the night and *he* hasn't caught him out, no-one will.'

Effigy shook his head.

'Not necessarily,' he said. 'There are ways and means to achieve these things, ways and means.'

'You have a plan?'

Effigy shrugged. 'I might. How often do you people meet up?'

'Not regularly enough,' said Obegarde. 'It's Burnie, you see. He can't get away during the day without the other council members suspecting he's up to something, and Jimmy can't do Thursday nights because he's gravedigging.'

'And I work virtually non-stop,' said Shably.

'Me too,' added Nazz. 'I'm demolishing the old schoolhouse on Royal Road tomorrow night.'

'OK,' Effigy said, pursing his lips and releasing a heavy sigh. 'You sound like a very disorganized rabble, and I have decided that I will take over as a *temporary* leader, but there have to be some changes. So let's get this straight: *I* will go away and devise a plan to find out once and for all whether Curfew is Curfew. All in agreement?'

There were some reluctant nods, but Burnie and Jimmy Quickstint looked particularly pleased with the decision.

'Very well, we'll all meet again in three days, by which time I will have everything we need to proceed. We'll meet at the stroke of nine outside the Crushload Inn on the harbour. No arguments. Good evening, gentlemen.'

Effigy bowed low, and departed.

CHAPTER
SEVEN

'Now,' said Viscount Curfew, striding back and forth across the throne room with his hands clasped firmly behind his back. 'I think I explained myself clearly, but do feel free to question anything you don't *completely* understand...'

The scribe, whose hands were still trembling, attempted to focus on the parchment before him.

'Y-you want me to ask the Rooftop Runners for a list of any assassins who might make good royal b-bodyguards.'

'Precisely.'

'-and then tell them that you want one with no moral fibre whatsoever, preferably one who is possessed, or an animal, or one who is totally oblivious to-'

'NO!' Curfew raced across the room, drew a blade from his belt hook and brought it to within an inch of the scribe's throat. 'You don't tell them the last part, and you certainly don't repeat what I've said to you word for word! You just ask for the list and individual case histories, and then you walk out of the building. You say NOTHING ELSE.'

The scribe moaned as he felt the blade edge bite into his neck.

'Are we clear, do you think?'

'Y-yes, Excellency. Absolutely crystal clear, Excellency.'

'Good man. Now get out of my sight.'

Curfew watched the scribe gather up his scrolls and leave; the wretch practically tripped over his own feet on the way out. He hadn't been gone more than a few seconds when the staff bell rang and a man Curfew recognised as one of the palace's junior guards hurried in.

'You'd better have a good reason for failing to knock,' said the viscount, sitting on the edge of his desk.

'Yes, Excellency. There's a big fight in the kitchen between two of the cooks. All hell's breaking loose and-'

'That's it? You disturb me because of a minor brawl? Why can't you sort it out?'

The guard swallowed a few times before continuing.

'Well, it's just that it was Vortas who started it, and he's only here for a few days on trial-leave from the gaol. Do I have your permission to eject him from the palace? He's been nothing but trouble, Excellency, and we can get him sent straight back to-'

'Trial leave from gaol?' Curfew repeated, his interest suddenly stirred. 'For what, exactly?'

'I'm sorry, Excellency?'

The viscount rolled his eyes.

'For what crime was Vortas incarcerated?'

'Oh, for poisoning, your Excellency. He killed the entire ground staff at Baroness Raggly's House in Legrash.'

'And you employed him here as a cook?'

The guard shook his head emphatically.

'Not me, Excellency: you made all hiring duties the job of the palace administrator, don't you rememb-'

'Don't QUESTION me, boy!'

The guard shrank away before Curfew's wrath.

'F-f-forgive me, Excellency. I d-didn't mean to-'

'I'll let it go this once,' the viscount said, moving around the desk and taking a seat behind it. 'Have the palace administrator thrown into the dungeons, then find young Vortas and bring him to me.'

'Y-yes, Excellency.'

As the guard dashed out into the corridor, Curfew gripped the arms of his seat and smiled cruelly. A poisoner, eh? That *will* come in handy.'

'It's MAGIC,' Groan spat, stepping back and raising his broadsword, 'an' magic is always bad news. We 'ave to smash it.'

'No!' yelled Gordo, stepping in front of the crystal ball to face off his friend. 'We're not going to destroy the ruddy thing when we don't even know what it is!'

'I agree,' said Gape, evenly. 'It'll probably be worth a mint in Legrash or Dullitch.'

Gordo nodded.

'D'you reckon that's where it's from?'

'I'm not sure,' Gape admitted, 'The stand looks funny. Should we try to lift it off or something?'

'Don' go near it,' Groan warned. 'Magic's always bad; 'specially them glass balls. 'S bound to be 'chanted.'

Gordo laughed.

'There's nothing in it, Groan! It's probably just a glass

sphere, a trinket like those ones the merchants are always touting!'

'Yes there is...' said Gape, quietly.

'You what?'

'There *is* something in there.'

Groan and Gordo both turned to look at Gape, who was staring wide-eyed at the crystal.

'Smash it,' boomed the giant barbarian, but his brother was already bending down to clasp the ball.

'I really wouldn't look at it if I were you,' said Gordo, his battleaxe suddenly hefted in both hands.

'I-I'm just looking.'

The two warriors watched as Gape's face twisted into a contorted smile.

'What can you see?' Gordo asked, impatiently.

Gape shrugged.

'A swirling mist,' he said. 'But it's moving, changing, forming into something.'

'Something good?' the dwarf hazarded.

'Hmm...I can't tell yet.'

'Well, keep looking. You don't appear to be suffering any ill effe-'

'Agghhhhhhhhhhhh!'

Gape screamed, his knees buckled and he collapsed against the wall. His hands - still tightly gripping the ball - were shaking and his eyes were practically bulging out of their sockets.

'Heeelp me! The pppaain! I c-can't let go of iiiitttt!'

His two companions moved like lightning; Gordo threw his axe aside and dropped to the floor, swinging his sturdy legs around and sweeping Gape off his feet. At the same time, Groan brought up an iron-like fist and punched the crystal ball out of his brother's hands. It flew through the air, hit the far wall...and shattered.

The chamber filled with a blistering light, the first beams of which struck the coffin and made it shake uncontrollably.

Gordo rolled himself into a ball and clasped both hands over his head, while Groan tried to use his broadsword to deflect the beams that danced around the room.

And then the light died...and there was nothing but silence.

∽

VISCOUNT CURFEW STAGGERED through the door to his private chamber, practically fell against a stand concealed in the corner of the room and snatched up the globe that rested atop it.

'M-master? What is it? I'm changing again! You said that-'

The hiss in the globe was low and quiet, though it sounded deafening in Curfew's ears.

'H-how is that possible? You concealed the clearing yourself!'

Again, the terrible hiss: more urgent, this time.

'B-broken? But that's part of our power conduit! The corpse will be revealed! C-can you sustain our deception with just one globe as a channel?'

The reply was almost threatening.

'Yes, Master, of course I'll take care of this one. If *this* were to break, we would have no way of-arghh! I know, Master, but you *have* to change me back. I will be powerless without the disguise...

Again, there was a pause. Then, a sharp bolt of lightning flashed from the globe...

~

'Well, that torch is good,' said Gordo, eventually, raising himself on his elbows. 'It's still going, look! Ha! Now that's what I call 'enchanted'.'

Groan nodded towards his fallen brother. 'Wass wrong wiv Gape?'

'Not sure,' said Gordo, struggling to his feet and waddling across the room. 'Maybe he hit his head on the way down.'

'Mmm...' said Groan, doubtfully. 'Or maybe tha' ball did it to 'im.'

Gordo checked for a pulse.

'Well, he's still breathing. He must just be asleep.' He leaned down so that his mouth was level with the barbarian's ear. 'Gape. Oi, Gape! GAPE, YOU MORON! WAKE UP!'

'I tol' ya that ball was trouble.'

'Yes, yes you did. And you were right; as usual. So what're we going to do now?'

Groan shrugged.

'Well, we've got tha' 'ammer to sell to Curfew-'

'I meant about your brother, you cold-hearted oaf!'

'Ah, right. Well, if we go an' sell tha' 'ammer in Dullitch, we can prob'ly sort Gape out while we're there.'

'What? How?'

'I dunno. Spec' we'll find a wizard or somefin'. We did las' time, 'member?'

'Yes, and look what happened to him! Let's just get Gape out of here, shall we?'

'Yeah, right. I'm takin' that chain, though.'

Groan stomped over to the coffin, went to reach inside...and paused.

'He's changed.'

'What?' said Gordo, still trying to shake Gape awake. 'Who's changed?'

'The corpse. It ain't the same bloke no more.'

'Eh?'

'This corpse: 's a different bloke in 'ere now.'

'Don't be ridiculous!'

'I ain't lyin'; come an' see!'

Gordo picked up his battleaxe and climbed the stone plinth.

'Great gods!' he said. 'It is, too! A totally different skeleton! And now the smell's about right: this one's starting to rot.' Gordo put his head on one side and studied the decayed form. 'I know it's going a bit, around the features,' he said. 'But who does that face remind you of?'

Groan carefully examined the peeling lips, the buckled nose and the hollowed-out eyes before he came to a conclusion.

'It looks like Uncle Charni.'

'No no no! Someone who's still alive! Doesn't it remind you of a certain nobleman we've met a few times?'

'Well, yeah,' said Groan immediately. 'It *looks* a bit like Viscount Curfew, only it can't be: he's livin'.'

Gordo nodded, heaved a sigh.

'You're sure the viscount's still alive, are you?'

'Yeah; I mean, we'd 'ave 'erd, wouldn' we? Me bein' king o' Phlegm an' all.'

'Hmm...you're right. Maybe it's just a coincidence. Still, this whole thing is pretty strange. That inn back there had a rotten feel to it and now this – an enchanted chapel in a deserted wood with a corpse that's under some sort of illusion spell, and an evil magic globe?'

Groan shrugged.

'Sounds' like a normal aft'noon to me.'

'Yes,' Gordo agreed. 'To *you* it would, but why would anyone bother to magically disguise a corpse?'

'Dunno.'

'Hmm…' Gordo sniffed a few times. 'Shall we get the hell out of here? Only, you'll have to carry Gape because there's no way I can.'

'Right,' said Groan, sheathing his broadsword and snatching up the enchanted torch. 'We 'ead for Dullitch, though; I wanna see what that 'ammer's worth…'

The pair slowly moved out of the room, Gape slung haphazardly over Groan's shoulder.

CHAPTER
EIGHT

'Oh, you're back, Excellency...' The guard looked embarrassed to find the throne room occupied. 'I, um, I brought Vortas Lythay to see you, but you disappeared-'

'Yes, and now I have returned: so send him in.'

The guard bowed low and did as he was instructed, leaving a thin, pale and spiteful-looking youth standing alone in the centre of the throne room.

'Vortas,' said Curfew, who still felt slightly uneasy about his recent transformation. 'What sort of a name is that?'

'It's Legrasian, Excellency,' Vortas confirmed, sniffing after every word. 'My father was Limplat Lythay, fourth in line to the Raggly Trading Empire. Unfortunately, I never got the fortune I deserved.'

Curfew smiled. 'Oh dear. Whatever happened?'

'My oldest brother inherited.'

'And you poisoned him?'

'Yes, Excellency, but then the fortune was passed down to my older sister...'

'Who you poisoned.'

'Yes, Excellency, but then my other brother...'

'...died of food poisoning.'

'Yes, which is when they arrested me...'

'...but not before you'd poisoned the entire Raggly House staff.'

'Payback, your Excellency: I felt it was deserved.'

'I agree.'

'You do?' Vortas looked up in surprise at this unprecedented response. 'Really?'

'Absolutely,' Curfew confirmed. 'I think you're a very talented young man and, in point of fact, I could use your services very well. How would you feel about a job higher up in the palace echelons? A job like, say, my personal assistant?'

'Oh yes, Excellency, I'd love to do that.'

'I'd start you on a salary of fifty crowns per week.'

'That's twice what I'm getting in the kitchens!' Vortas exclaimed, quickly clapping a hand over his mouth in the event that he'd made a terrible mistake in revealing the fact.

'Quite. Your basic duties would involve reading, writing, playing games, chasing any maid you care to set an eye upon...and, occasionally, poisoning my guests.'

There was a moment of awkward silence.

'Y-you want me to poison people?'

'Yes.'

'And you're going to pay me to do it?'

'Correct.'

'Can I watch?'

'I beg your pardon?' Curfew suddenly straightened himself in the seat; he hadn't expected the question. 'What do you mean?'

Vortas sniffed again.

'Will I get to watch the results of my work, Excellency?'

Curfew thought about this for a second.

'If you wish,' he said, after a time. 'That is, as long as you do your job well.'

'Oh, I will, Excellency,' said Vortas, gleefully rubbing his hands together. 'I will. Is there anything you'd like me to do right now?'

'Yes,' said the viscount, quietly. 'I'd like you to sit down: I'm going to tell you a secret.'

Vortas obediently took a seat while Curfew began to speak.

'I can read minds, Mister Lythay, and yours – though determined to succeed – seems very...loyal. You must understand, however, that the information I'm about to give you will inevitably result in your death should you...happen to leak it. And I do not poison easily.'

Vortas looked momentarily terrified but managed a smile nonetheless.

'Mister Lythay,' Curfew continued, rising from his seat and moving down the steps towards him. He sat beside the poisoner and leaned very close to his ear. 'Who do you think I am?'

Vortas turned and looked into the ruler's eyes.

'You're Viscount Curfew,' he said. 'Lord of Dullitch.'

Curfew nodded sagely, and whispered: 'You got the last bit right.'

'GOBLINS,' said Gordo, peering out from the edge of the Beanstalk woods. 'Hundreds of them: moving west in a warband.'

Groan dumped his brother's motionless body on the grass.

'Le' me see,' he said, yanking at a branch that obscured his view. ''s not 'undreds, is it? An' the chief looks weak...'

'I know,' admitted Gordo. 'But still, I don't think we should get involved, do you? What with Gape unconscious an' all.'

'Gape's never no 'elp 'nyway. I'm gonna go an' 'ave 'em down. Goblins 'as always got loot on 'em.'

'NO!' Gordo jumped up and down on the spot. 'Listen to me; if we attack them, one of us – undoubtedly me - will have to stand here and protect Gape.'

'Why?'

'In case they kill him!'

'You reckon?'

'Of course! So that means you'll be taking on thirty goblins.'

'Yeah: shall I tie an 'and b'ind me back?'

'Very funny. Seriously, Groan, I don't think we should attack, regardless of how much robbed loot they might be carrying.'

The giant barbarian frowned.

'Wha' do we do, then?'

'Mmm?'

'We jus' gonna let 'em pass?'

'Yes! Haven't you ever done that before: just let things pass without violently attacking them?'

'Nah.'

'Unbelievable.'

'An' I ain't gonna nex' time.'

'Fine. Your decision; we'll just agree to let these goblins off *this* time: for *me*.'

'Yeah.' Groan listened to the rhythmic march of the scraggly warband. 'Nah,' he said. 'I've 'ad second foughts, an' I don't get 'em often.' And, booming a war cry, he erupted from his hiding place and hacked the goblin chief's head off.

Gordo felt like sobbing but decided to teach Groan a lesson instead. Marching away from the sounds of battle, he grabbed hold of Gape's heavy boots and dragged the warrior towards Chudderford.

CHAPTER
NINE

The clock struck ten, and several of the Crushload Inn's more unwelcome customers were ejected onto the pavement.

'Do you know what time it is?' Effigy snapped, when Jimmy Quickstint finally appeared in the alley beside the inn. 'I've been freezing my eyebrows off out here waiting for you!'

Jimmy shrugged. 'Sorry; we got talking.'

'Never mind,' muttered Effigy, coldly. 'I don't suppose it matters in the greater scheme of things. Where are the rest of 'em?'

'Well,' Jimmy began, looking sheepish. 'Burnie couldn't come; he got summoned to some last-minute dinner at the palace, but everyone else is here.'

'Eh?' Effigy peered around him. 'Everyone else is *where*? I can't see anybody, can you?'

'They're inside, Mr Spatula: in the pub. We've been here since nine o'clock.'

'Yes,' said Effigy, resentfully checking his pocket watch. 'So have I.'

Inside, the Crushload was heaving. Pirates knocked seven bells out of each other, while assassins drove blades between ribs and merchants whispered trade deals in some of the shadier corners.

Effigy walked straight past the table containing the Secret Army of Dullitch, calling out 'Follow me' as he went and pointing towards the bar. A barely conceivable nod at the landlord saw the bar-top lifted, and Effigy quickly disappeared through a door behind it.

The others followed, rather awkwardly behind him, expecting to get stopped at some point and, possibly, searched.

Fortunately, both expectations were proved wrong.

'In here,' said Effigy, opening a door and allowing the group to filter in and take their places at a table identical to the one in the Ferret.

When everyone was seated, Effigy took the top chair and three deep breaths.

'Excuse me,' said Obegarde, trying and failing to keep the sarcasm out of his voice. 'But this room looks very familiar.'

'It's no different from the Ferret,' said Nazz, doubtfully.

'No different at all,' Obegarde agreed.

'In point of fact, it's *very* different,' Effigy said, tapping a fingernail on the tabletop. 'Firstly, because it's not the most famous drinking pit in Dullitch and, secondly, because it's *incredibly* close to the palace and very well concealed by being on the harbour front! It's absolutely perfect for these meetings, and, possibly, a more secure venue. I'm not sure I trust that Ripple. But if you're worried about offending him, don't be: you can still hold all your fake "Royal Society of Lantern Collectors" gatherings there. How's that?'

There were a few surprised stares and several enthusiastic murmurs of approval.

'I must admit, I'm impressed,' said Obegarde, eventually. 'If your plans are as good as your venue-scouting, we should have Curfew's impostor off the throne in no time.'

'Yes, well let's not start congratulating each other too early, gentlemen. We still have a long way to go...'

Obegarde nodded. 'Agreed, but, as it happens, I've actually had a thought...'

Effigy raised an eyebrow. 'Oh?'

'Well, last year, when we were investigating Curfew's kidnap, Jimmy and I almost sneaked into the palace through the sewers. Couldn't we try that again?'

'No,' said Effigy, shaking his head. 'Absolutely not, and the reason is that we're not actually trying to sneak into the palace. We're *trying* to get a free run of the place.'

'What?' said Nazz, gruffly. 'But that's impossible, isn't it?'

'Totally impossible,' Shably finished.

'Nothing is totally impossible,' said Effigy, sternly. 'It's all about how you approach these things. We *will* gain entrance to the palace and we *will* have free run of the place because we will look and sound like palace guards...and high-ranking ones, at that.'

'Get out,' said Jimmy Quickstint, a manic grin on his face. 'You're three sheets to the wind, you are.'

Effigy's face muscles didn't move.

'I'm absolutely serious,' he said.

'And how do you plan to pull off this miraculous illusion?' asked Obegarde.

'Um...by way of a miraculous illusion, actually.'

All eyes turned to face Effigy Spatula.

'Good, I'm glad I have everyone's attention. This afternoon, while you were all diligently going about your business, I broke into the palace's administering office on North Street and perused the files for all the viscount's senior officers. I also popped into the illegal magic emporium beneath the tailor's on Burrow Street and stole some of this.'

Effigy grinned as he deposited two pouches on the tabletop. 'Any questions?'

'What is it?' said Jimmy, doubtfully, opening the first pouch to reveal its contents.

'Shaping dust,' replied Obegarde, without blinking. 'You use it to help create the illusion that you're someone else.'

'Like those two soldiers,' added Nazz, his two fangs gleaming in the candlelight.

'You catch on quickly, for an ogre,' said Effigy, trying to keep the patronising tone from his voice.

'I'm afraid the plan is flawed,' said Obegarde, leaning back in his chair and sighing, despondently. 'In order to transfigure yourself, you need a hair or skin sample from the subject in question...and I'm fairly certain you won't have managed *that* in a few days?'

'No,' Effigy admitted, '*I* haven't...but our good friend Mr Shably will.'

Brim looked up. 'Me?'

'Yes.'

'You want me to steal a hair from two of the top soldiers in the palace? Do you have any idea how difficult that will be?'

'Yes. Almost impossible, I would imagine.'

'Ha! Try absolutely, totally, one hundred percent impossible! If I get caught doing that stuff, I'll get a swift execution...and then you people won't have anybody inside the palace to report back to you.'

Effigy nodded.

'Whereas we currently have somebody at the palace who's too frightened to actually eavesdrop on the subject anyway?'

'Now, hang on a minute-'

'We don't *have* a minute, Mr Shably: we have all the time in the world. Time enough for you to plot, plan and cleverly design the method of your infiltration.'

'But you'll need them out of the palace for this plan to work anyway!'

'Agreed; they will need to be kidnapped. Nazz can probably handle that...'

'Right, so why don't you just take the hairs when you've kidnapped them?'

'Because the potion will take a good few hours to work and we don't want to hold on to the officers longer than we need to, otherwise we'll get found out!'

'We'll probably get found out anyway!' Shably yelled. 'It's the worst plan I've ever heard!'

Effigy rolled his eyes. 'I'm sure you'll get the samples we need with the minimum of fuss. Three cheers for Mr Shably! Hip Hip-'

Three rather stilted 'hoorays' were eventually forced out of the audience.

'Good show. Now all we need is two willing volunteers to swallow the mixture when it's prepared. Unfortunately, Nazz is ruled out because of his superior size, so I suggest Obegarde and Mr Quickstint.

Jimmy nodded knowingly, and said: 'It just had to be me, didn't it?'

Effigy smiled. 'Yes, I'm afraid it did: your discretion is practically *legend* in this city. You're the thief who-I'm sorry, why is everyone laughing? If we're to pull off this little series of operations, we need to...er...WHERE IS HE?'

The rest of the group stopped sniggering and turned blank stares on their new leader.

'WHERE DID YOU SAY HE WAS?' Effigy repeated, his face suddenly ashen.

He was looking straight at Jimmy.

'Who?' said the thief nervously.

'You said that Burnie couldn't make it tonight because he'd been called to a last-minute dinner: where?'

Jimmy swallowed.

'At the palace.'

'And you didn't think anything of that?'

'Well, no. It's just a council thing-'

'What if Curfew has found out about the group?' 'He can't have: how-'

'But what if he *has*...?'

'You think Ripple might have betrayed us?' said Obegarde, doubtfully. 'I really don't think old Rorgrim would-'

'He would for a stack of crowns or a Late Opening Licence,' Jimmy added. 'And I don't know about the money, but he's certainly got a Late Opening Licence: he was telling me how it came through yesterday morning...'

'Fantastic!' Obegarde snapped. 'So what do we do n-'

Effigy clapped his hands and motioned for silence.

'We wait until the morning; it's the only thing we can do. If Burnie doesn't return, I'll decide what to do then.'

'Of course he'll return,' Nazz growled. 'Burnie's been on the council since the rat catastrophe. Curfew trusts him.'

'But I thought the whole point of this group was to prove

that Curfew isn't Curfew...and if that's *true*, who's to say what'll happen?'

A kind of terror gripped the table.

'Worry not,' Effigy assured them. 'I'll find out exactly what's going on.' He turned to Nazz. 'In the meantime, big guy, I need you to go on an important mission for me.'

'Me?' The ogre's blank expression lightened a little. 'What do you want me to do?'

Effigy grinned.

'I've arranged for some *friends* to visit us. They're coming from Little Irkesome, and as I don't particularly want them *declared* when they enter the city, I'd like you to intercept their coach and bring them in using a more discreet route. Do you think you're up to that?'

The ogre beamed back at him.

'Hey, they don't call me Fetcher for nothing...' he said.

'No,' Effigy agreed. 'They don't call you Fetcher at *all*, do they?'

'Not really, no.'

'Well do shut up then, and go find a cart. As for the rest of you; we'll meet back here in three days' time...and that's all of us: *including* Burnie, hopefully...'

There were a few vague nods before the secret army got up to leave.

'Oh, and I nearly forgot,' Effigy called out. 'Obegarde. Can you swim?'

The vampire spun around, a quizzical look on his face. 'I can if the need arises. Why?'

Effigy shrugged.

'I might need you to row a boat for me in a few days' time, that's all.'

~

THE TABLE WAS enormous and ludicrously overstocked for the three people that sat huddled at one end.

'What are we doing here, exactly?' said Rin Lye, Dullitch Council's most senior judge.

'Not much if I know Curfew,' Taciturn Cadrick replied, picking carefully at his pork chop. 'He's probably poisoned the food. Hahaha!'

'I doubt that, somehow,' said Burnie. 'This is the first meeting he's called since his kidnap: he probably just wants to make sure everything is still running smoothly at City Hall. Still, I'm certainly not hungry.'

'Well, I am!' The vice-chairman smiled, popping a square of the meat into his mouth and giving it an experimental chew.

'Good evening, senior councillors,' said a voice from the far end of the room.

Viscount Curfew strode into the dining hall and took a seat next to Burnie, making the three colleagues very uncomfortable indeed.

'I do hope I haven't kept you from any important business, this evening,' he said.

'Of course not, Excellency,' said Rin Lye, diplomatically.

'A visit with you is always a pleasure, Excellency,' Taciturn added.

'And you, Mister Chairman, I haven't torn you away from any pressing engagements?'

Burnie drank from his wine glass and shrugged.

'I could've done with the night off, but apart from that...'

Curfew's expression changed immediately to a sneer,

while the remaining councillors shook their heads in an effort to distance themselves from their chief.

'I'm sorry I bothered you, really I am,' Curfew went on. 'But I did feel that a meeting between us was long overdue. After all, together we do govern the city; do we not?'

Burnie nodded. 'We do, Excellency. Was it that little detail you wanted to talk to us about?'

Curfew grinned. 'Yes. Absolutely. But shall we discuss it over by the fire? It's so draughty in here.'

Burnie shrugged. 'That never seemed to bother you before, Excellency.'

'Well, it does now. Hmm...have you all finished your wine?'

'Yes.'

'Lovely body on it.'

'Good year, Excellency.'

'Very well.' Curfew ushered them over to the great chairs beside the fire and himself strode up to stand beside the roaring inferno. 'In that case, I'll tell you something very interesting: I have a rather important announcement to make.'

Burnie suddenly sat up in his chair.

'Now, I know that Viscount Curfew allowed you all to run the city as you saw fit...but I am not Viscount Curfew. My name is Sorrell Diveal, Noble Lord of Illmoor, and as such I bow to no man. Therefore, you can consider yourselves on a permanent leave of absence.'

Taciturn and Rin Lye were both gasping for breath, partly out of shock but mostly because a deadly poison was beginning to take hold of them. Rin Lye was the first to lose consciousness, but the council's deputy chairman wasn't far behind her.

Burnie began to rise from his chair.

'Sorrell Diveal,' he said. 'So THAT'S who you are. I did wonder.'

Diveal's evil grin froze on his face.

'You suspected something? Ha! Impressive, for a creature that appears to be constructed entirely of candle wax. I'm impressed.'

The little troglodyte shrugged.

'Oh, I doubt you are, Mr Diveal. How did you pull it off? Did you kill Curfew in those woods during the rescue and then swap places with him? Yes, I bet that's it. Hmm...one thing *does* interest me, though: are you doing all this on your own steam or do you have magical assistance?'

Diveal said nothing.

'Either way...' Burnie went on. 'I should warn you, as your plans were so well orchestrated, that I haven't eaten any of the food your servants brought in this evening...'

Diveal's grin mutated into a sneer.

'I didn't think you would,' he whispered. 'That's why I poisoned the wine as well.'

Burnie smiled, weakly. 'Good thinking,' he said, and fell forward, clutching his stomach.

'Oh, I'm known for it,' Diveal said, sidestepping the little troglodyte, who was now snatching his throat and trying to fight the burgeoning pain.

'Y-you'll never get away with this – not in the long run. There are those who will s-stop you...'

Diveal shrugged.

'I do not doubt that there are those who will try,' he said.

Burnie made to reply and then fell silent, his struggles at an end.

'Very good.' Diveal finished, prodding the dead creature

with the toe of his boot. 'A swift and accurate poison: I commend you, Mr Lythay...'

In the furthest corner of the room, a figure emerged from the shadows.

'A job well done,' said Vortas, his eyes filled with glee. 'Even if I do say so myself! I poisoned the wine, the food, the bread, the salt *and* the pepper. I even sprayed the base of the glasses; so they couldn't even lick their fingers without risk! It really was a treat to watch the little creature avoiding the main meal. A treat! Hahahahaha!'

Diveal's face darkened.

'Don't be too quick to cheer your own efforts, Mister Lythay,' he said. 'Nevertheless, you can consider your 'trial' run successful: you now have a permanent post.'

'Many thanks; I can assure you that you *won't* be disappointed.'

'I better not be.'

'Can I just ask one question?'

'I suppose so.' Diveal waited. 'Well?'

'Why did you want to kill them all? Two of them seemed almost sycophantic...'

Diveal put his head on one side and studied the poisoner. 'Not that it's any of your business,' he began. 'But I killed them because they were in my way...and that's what happens to people who get in my way: they die. In that respect, we have a lot in common.' He cast a quick glance around the room. 'Now listen; I want you to go and find some body bags: we'll need those to transport our three departed friends.'

'Yes, Master. What-'

'You can dump them in the river...but remember to take them OUT of the bags before you do that. Oh, and be sure to dismiss the sentries outside: we don't want them seeing anything that might cause interest. Hmm...and DO stop licking your lips, Vortas – there's something deeply unsettling about the way you amuse yourself.'

The poisoner bowed low, and departed, his eerie cackle echoing through the chamber.

Diveal smiled inwardly, marched over to the dining table and sat down to finish his own meal, though he was careful to check it first. After a few mouthfuls, he was so engrossed in his thoughts that he failed to notice a small shadow rising on the other side of the room.

'Don't know much about troglodytes, do you?' said a voice. Diveal looked up, sharp. 'You see, as far as poisons are concerned, we're pretty much a lost cause. Oh, we might *look* exactly like big-nosed goblins, but we just don't have their bloodstream...'

The troglodyte was waddling towards him, a strangely jagged sword in his hand.

'I call this blade Roughcut: a wizard I knew gave it to me as a present just before he retired from the council. I'm told it's pretty good.'

Diveal's smile almost split his face in two.

'It'll need to be,' he said. 'Because I *will* kill you.'

'You have to,' Burnie admitted. 'Because if I get out of this room alive, I'll tell the entire city who you really are...and I'll personally see to it that what's left of the council removes you.'

'Ha! You'd need *every* remaining councillor to approve such a move...and none of them will believe you.'

Diveal rose from the chair, threw off his coat and drew his own blade.

'While we're on the subject of swords,' he said, carefully

rounding the table. 'This one originally belonged to Edwyn Vitkins. It should have been mine after that, but I had to watch both Modeset *and* his idiot nephew wield it first.'

'Ha! My heart bleeds for y-'

Burnie's words were cut short as Diveal rocketed over a chair and lunged at him...but the troglodyte had turned aside.

Steel clashed as Burnie brought his own blade to bear against the impostor's longsword.

Teeth clenched and eyes flashing with malice, Diveal drove his blade down hard, forcing the little creature against the table.

Burnie twitched as he was pushed back: the impostor's strength was unbelievable.

'Die, you little maggot,' Diveal growled, his hands beginning to glow as if charged by lightning. 'Die! Die! Die!'

Burnie felt the table edge against his neck and smiled. In a split second, he ducked his head down and rolled backwards, slashing at Diveal's legs as he came up beneath the table.

'Argghhh!'

Diveal's cry of pain at the wound carved across his shins was followed by a cry of rage as he dived forward and smashed the table aside as if he was brushing away a piece of parchment.

The table flew against the far wall and splintered, but Burnie had already gone.

The troglodyte dashed across the room as fast as his little legs would carry him. He used a chair to spring onto the viscount's desk, then took a run up and leaped, wildly towards the oval window of the office. In a shower of glass, Burnie the troglodyte left the palace.

There was a second of silence, followed by a distant splash.

And Sorrell Diveal screamed with rage.

The door flew open behind him.

'Master! What's happened?' said Lythay, dropping the bags in the doorway and hurrying over to Diveal, who was almost incandescent with fury.

'The troglodyte was alive, fool! They're immune to poisons!'

'I-I didn't know, Master! We'll find him at once-'

'NO! Let him go.'

'Master?'

'You heard me. I want you to send a squad to the council offices, instead. Tell them that the council is under suspicion of treason and that they are to arrest EVERYONE in residence there. If Burnie returns to the offices, they are to kill him on sight.'

'Yes, Master.'

'Go now, and be sure to tell the City Criers that an attempt has been made on the life of Viscount Curfew. The troglodyte is now an Enemy of State.'

BURNIE HAD NEVER BEEN MORE grateful for his ability to swim. This, combined with his extensive knowledge of the palace grounds and the lay of the city outside, saw him safely into a shallow waterway that, in turn, bled into the dockland wash.

He floated for a time, then began to use his hands and feet to direct himself towards the nearest turn-off.

The city was dark and shadowy tonight, and any guard patrols would be easy to avoid.

One thing was certain: he couldn't return to City Hall: they would be waiting for him. He *had* to get *out* of Dullitch fast, even if it meant not being able to tell the others that he was safe. A fast horse would be needed. If only he could get a message of some kind to Effigy...

If only.

High above, a lone bat flapped through the air. Unwittingly, it gave Burnie an idea.

CHAPTER
TEN

Time passed, and there was still no sign of Groan, but Gordo wasn't overly concerned. He'd managed to reach Chudderford, where he'd booked himself on a dwarf barge that had crossed the River Washin without incident (if you didn't count the fact that Gape had made one monotonous snore last the entire journey). Once in Little Irkesome, he'd bought two tickets on a fast coach to Dullitch: a coach that had unexpectedly turned out to contain two assassins. Still, considering the area, it was probably a good thing to have trained killers on board: the coach was rattling its way through Mostang, Illmoor's largest and most legendary cemetery. Gordo had heard some truly horrible stories about people who'd spent the night there and been confronted with various avatars of the damned. To make matters (and his imagination) worse, it was very early in the morning and a mist was beginning to settle on the land.

'Sweet?' said the young but nevertheless shady-looking character opposite him.

Gordo shook his head. 'No thanks, I'm dieting.'

'Ah,' said the assassin. 'Have you tried Weightshrinkers?'
'No, what's that?'
'Oh, it's this cracking new points system devised by the boffins at the Royal College in Legrash. I'm on it at the moment: trying to shape myself up for my fifth kill.'

Gordo frowned. 'But you're eating sweets!'

'Yes, but they're really low on points: besides, the whole thing is relative to your lifestyle. Take me, for instance: I always work my food off. If I'm assassinating someone and it's a rooftop job, I get to earn a few extra points for the d-'

'GORDO GOLDEXE,' said the dwarf, before any long stories were started. 'Please to meet you.'

'Victor Franklin, likewise. Is the big guy with you?'
'Yep.'
'He looks tired. Didn't get much sleep last night, huh?'
Gordo rolled his eyes.

'Oh he got sleep all right,' he said. 'And the night before and the night before that. He's been sleeping non-stop for days.'

'I've got an aunt like that,' said Victor, knowingly. 'Erm...would you like me to introduce you to my friend?'

Gordo took a look at the remaining assassin and smiled doubtfully.

'This is Mifkindle Green,' said Victor, not taking the hint.

The young man sitting next to him looked every inch the bespectacled geek. Apart from anything else, his trousers were several inches too short and his glasses were joined in the middle with what appeared to be part of a bandage. He was toying with a twelve-sided dice.

'You're an assassin, too, are you?' Gordo hazarded.

Mifkindle grinned.

'F-f-for my s-sins,' he complained. 'I'm th-th-thinking of g-giving it up, though-'

Gordo sniffed. 'Really? Is the work too tough for you?'

'Are you kidding?' Victor laughed. 'How many kills have you got under your belt now, Mif? It must be five hundred!'

'Five hundred and s-s-six,' Mifkindle said, tiredly. 'But I'm pretty b-bored with the whole s-s-scene, to be honest.'

'YOU'VE KILLED FIVE HUNDRED AND SIX PEOPLE?' Gordo exclaimed. *Hells bells*, he thought to himself, *Groan's only up to three hundred, himself. This young bloke must be death on legs.* 'You must be very proud of yourself,' he said aloud.

'No, n-not at all. I hate k-killing people; I only ever d-d-do it under duress and I'm *always* in t-two minds about whether it's the *right* thing to d-d-do. Take my last k-kill, for instance: there I was with a n-noose around this fellow's n-n-neck and I'm thinking, shall I or shan't I...and all the while this g-guy's s-spluttering around trying to tell me that we're b-both on the edge of this ch-chasm-'

'NICE DAY, ISN'T IT?' said Gordo, loudly, hoping and praying that either Groan would catch up with them or that Gape would suddenly shake off the spell. Unfortunately, neither happened.

'What's your business in Dullitch then, Guido?'

'It's Gordo,' Gordo corrected. 'And I'm going to do some trade, and hopefully get my friend here back on his feet.'

'Oh, right. Good luck with that, then. You trading anything interesting?'

'Nah, just this old hammer.'

The dwarf grinned and pointed at the tool hanging from his belt.

'It's a bit r-rusted up, isn't it?' said Mifkindle, the mass murderer. 'Do you really th-think you can g-get anything for it?'

Gordo shook his head.

'Nah, but it's always worth a try. What about you two? On business, I suppose?'

Victor nodded.

'We've been hired in to-'

'Shh! Don't tell p-p-people that!' Mifkindle admonished, shaking a finger at his friend. He turned to Gordo. 'Let's just s-say it's a w-working holiday.'

'Right,' said Gordo, knowingly. 'Say no more.'

Please gods, he thought to himself, *let this journey end soon*.

As if in answer to his prayer, a pack of glutton ghouls suddenly erupted from the ground ahead and streamed toward the coach.

~

It was early morning in Dullitch; so early, in fact, that half the populace were still asleep.

Effigy Spatula threaded his way among the empty market stalls and stopped at a shop doorway that contained two hanging baskets, a dead rat and Brim Shably, who looked awkward out of his guard uniform.

'Anything?' Effigy asked, an expression of concern on his face.

'You mean apart from the wanted posters all over the place?' Shably hazarded. 'No, nothing yet. None of the junior guards 've seen hide nor hair of Burnie *or* the other two councillors who were invited in with him. All anyone knows is that Burnie tried something against the viscount and now he's top of the city's Most Wanted. As for the other two, well,

I reckon Curfew – the other Curfew, I mean – has done 'em all in. Do you think Burnie will contact us?'

Effigy stroked his beard.

'I wouldn't,' he admitted. 'Especially considering that the guards are all over City Hall, but I guess we shall see. Did you get the things I asked you to get from the anti-herbalist?'

'Yes: I've got two packets of head-lice and a pair of scissors.'

'Good stuff. Now listen, carefully, because I'm only going to say this once. I need you to plant these head-lice in the combs of your senior officers. Then, when the outbreak is revealed, I want you to offer to cut their hair for them.'

'That's the plan? Are you serious?'

'Of course I'm serious. I assume the senior officers we've targeted both have hair?'

'No, actually Brigadier Lanslide is almost bald...'

'Damn it! That's going to cause us problems!'

Shably sighed. 'Oh, don't worry. I'll...er...I'll think of something...'

'Like what?'

'Oh, I don't know...he *does* have a very large moustache. But listen, wouldn't it be easier just to take the hair from the combs?'

Effigy shook his head.

'No! We'll never get enough that way; besides, we won't be sure it's actually *their* own hair if you don't cut it from them yourself.'

Shably rubbed his chin.

'Well, all right, but I think-'

'Yes?'

'Won't it look a bit odd for a senior guard to suddenly offer his services as a hairdresser?'

Effigy stopped dead in the street, closed his eyes and counted to ten. Then he opened them again.

'I can't think of everything,' he snapped. 'Just do as you're told and get a hair sample from both of them.'

Shably sighed.

'Right. Fine; I'll do my best,' he said, wearily.

'Of course you will. Listen, I promise not to involve you in this matter *any further* once your task is done.'

Shably looked at the freedom fighter, hopefully.

'Not at all?'

'That's right; you do this one thing and, as far as I'm concerned, your part in the conspiracy has been played out in full.'

Effigy gave the tired soldier a companionable pat on the back and headed off in the direction of the Rotting Ferret.

'Undead! Undead! Argghhh!'

Ghouls descended on the coach like vultures on a corpse, spilling over each other in a frenzied effort to be the first of the pack to draw blood.

The coach, its driver having been the first hit by the volley of hurled human skulls, hurtled off the road and smashed into the side of a sturdy mausoleum.

Gordo shook himself to stop his head thudding. Then he drew his battleaxe, flung the coach door wide and leaped out, practically slicing one of the squat creatures in two before he'd even hit the ground. Following a speedy forward roll, he picked himself up and brought the great axe down again, removing several limbs in his attempt to check that Gape was still alive inside the coach. Fortunately, the big barbarian's chest was still moving rhythmically up and down.

Mifkindle Green was a blur; he'd produced what looked like a kitchen knife from the folds of his robe and was moving the blade so fast that several of the ghouls looked most alarmed when they suddenly fell apart without realising what'd hit them. His friend, Victor, was a good deal slower but still showed remarkable skill for a youngster: Gordo was almost tempted to ditch his mercenary career and join the pair of them. Even so, the trio was totally outmanned by the glutton ghouls, whose fat little legs, razor-sharp teeth and honed ability to tunnel were giving them the upper hand. Plus, there were literally *hundreds* of them.

Gordo swung his axe in a wild arc, then quickly twisted around and completed a full wheel, driving the ravenous little creatures back.

Unfortunately, Mifkindle and Victor were running out of steam: they'd both strayed too far from the coach and were caught in the centre of a widening circle of ghouls, valiantly fighting off each one that dashed towards them with increasingly exhausted stabs.

Then help arrived: a cart came thundering through the mist and ploughed straight into the ghouls, sending them flying in every direction. The driver, a creature of immense size, whom Gordo at first took to be Groan, leaped down from the roof-seat, produced a hefty-looking club and began to systematically pummel the remaining corpse-eaters into oblivion. The assassins quickly joined in and, together with Gordo's death-spinning battleaxe, they managed to completely turn the tide of the battle, driving the hungry creatures back below ground in the end.

'Th-thanks,' said Mifkindle, breathlessly. 'We r-r-really owe you one.'

'Don't mention it,' said Nazz, pulling back his hood to reveal an outsized head with a bulbous nose and two ivory white fangs. 'As a matter of fact, I'm here to collect you boys.'

Victor and Mifkindle shared a glance.

'Really?' said the former. 'You work with Effigy?'

'I do indeed. Mr Spatula didn't want you lads entering Dullitch the normal way, so he sent me out here to collect you. A good job, too; by the looks of it. Who's your friend?'

'F-friend?' said Mifkindle, peering around. 'Oh, that's G-g-gordo; he's a d-d-dwarf.'

Nazz rolled his eyes. 'Really?'

'I know; hard to believe, isn't it?' said Gordo.

'He's been travelling with us since Little Irkesome,' Victor explained. 'He has a sick companion with him, too.'

'Ah.' Nazz nodded. 'You going to Dullitch as well?'

'I was,' said Gordo resentfully, prodding the dead driver with the edge of his boot. 'Before the coach service packed up.'

'Can we t-take them along?' Mifkindle enquired.

Nazz shrugged.

'I don't see why not,' he said. 'We're going to have to sneak in anyway.'

'Thanks,' said Gordo, doubtfully. 'I'll just fetch Gape. Would you mind giving me a hand?'

Nazz nodded, and followed Gordo to the crashed coach.

'Can I ask you a question?' said the dwarf, leaning in to grab Gape's legs in the hope that the ogre would take the majority of his companion's weight.

'Depends,' said Nazz, loftily. 'What is it?'

'Well, why do you need to sneak back into the city? You've got Dullitch-issue plates on that cart of yours!'

'Mind your own business,' Nazz advised. 'I don't mean to be rude but, believe me, you don't want any part of what *we're* up to.'

'That bad, is it?'

'That bad.'

Gordo drew in a breath.

'Fine,' he said. 'Forget I asked; my friend and I are grateful for the lift anyway.'

They both loaded Gape onto the back of the cart while Mifkindle and Victor took a seat on the front.

'Mind if I ask a question of my own?' Nazz enquired.

'Go right ahead.'

'What actually happened to this fella?'

Gordo grinned. 'He's in an enchanted sleep.'

'How did *that* happen?'

'Oh, he broke some magic crystal ball; probably an evil wizard or a crazed necromancer behind it all, somewhere.'

'Isn't there always?'

Gordo laughed.

'Always is.'

Nazz and Gordo climbed onto the cart and the ogre took the reins, urging the horses into a brisk trot.

Morning was beginning to creep lazily over the landscape.

'So you're an ogre?' Gordo said conversationally, noting that the two assassins were deep in discussion. 'If you don't mind me saying, it's unusual to meet one of your sort with the ability to speak sentences...'

'Ha!'

'No offence...'

'None taken,' said Nazz, with a reassuring nod. 'On the whole, us ogres have always been a fighting race, but we're really much more civilized these days...'

'Seriously?'

'Oh yes. I mean, you've only got to look at the big cities: they're *full* of ogres. Most of them are merchant bodyguards or hired-swords, but there are a good few academics out there, too. Ogres have much more in common with humans than, say, trolls or hobgoblins.'

Gordo nodded. 'Come to think of it, I've never actually fought an ogre...'

'You don't want to; we can be really mean.'

'I'm sure,' said Gordo, sniffing. 'But I'm a mercenary and we never back down from a challenge.'

'Ha! You weren't doing too great back there though, were you?'

'That's not the same!' Gordo snapped. 'Undead don't count; they're a completely different kettle of fish.'

'What, you mean the kind you don't like to boil up in case it burns you? Hahahahaha!'

Gordo didn't want to concede a point, but the ogre's laugh was infectious and he soon found himself chuckling along with him.

'Yeah, well – I admit we might've got a bit out of our depth with that lot, but I'm still a damn good fighter.'

'Agreed,' said Nazz. 'I saw some of your axe work as I arrived: very impressive.'

'Thanks. I'm Captain of the Guard up at Phlegm, and I'm also in a gang of mercenaries: not that I'm the prime fighter, mind; I'm more your thinking warrior.'

'Ah.' Nazz nodded. 'Who's the big bad wolf in your group then; the other bloke?'

'Who, Gape?' Gordo shook his head. 'Gape's a tough one and no mistake, but it's his brother they all fear.'

The ogre nodded.

'Anyone I'd have heard of?'

'Groan Teethgrit.'

'Really?' Nazz took a breath and urged the cart forward. 'I'm assuming you mean Groan Teethgrit as in the barbarian king of Phlegm.'

'I do.'

'Wow: that's some company you keep, little friend.'

'Yeah,' Gordo nodded. 'It's not all a bed of roses, though...'

Nazz sniffed. 'Had a big falling out, did you?'

'Sort of. He went off to fight a goblin warband and, despite my pleading, left me alone to protect Gape. So I decided to just keep walking and leave him to it...'

'...and here you are!' Nazz finished, his fangs gleaming. 'How far back did you leave him?'

'Just outside Beanstalk Woods.'

'Damn! That's a long way to walk: hahahahaha!'

Gordo nodded. 'Oh, I'm sure he's cursing my name for it.'

'STINKIN' dwarves; ruddy waste o' space, the lot of 'em.'

Groan Teethgrit tramped along the dusty roads of Chudderford. Since his fight with the goblin-horde several days before, he'd had a succession of tavern brawls, all of which had ended in his favour, and he'd almost earned enough from the six arm-wrestling contests he'd won to buy a good horse.

Almost, but not quite...

Groan stopped in his tracks. He wasn't the best reader in Illmoor, but he recognised the word "Orse" when he saw it.

'Ere,' he shouted at a young boy who was scraping mud off his shoe on the far side of the street. 'You wanna earn a crown?'

The boy sauntered over, looking doubtful.

'What would I have to do?'

Groan pointed a finger. 'Read the sign on that door.'

The boy nodded, and Groan paid him. Then he squinted up at the sign.

'It says: "'Orse for sale. Chud' Shire. Good runner: Spittle to Legrash in two hours. Fifty crowns o.n.o. Ask round the back."'

Groan frowned.

'What's o.n.o. mean?'

The boy shrugged.

'I think it stands for One Nice Owner.'

The big barbarian nodded.

'Don't s'pose you know how long it takes to ge' from Legrash to Spittle?'

'Ten days, isn't it?'

'Yeah,' said Groan. 'I fort it was.' And with that, he stomped around to the back of the house.

The boy waited for him to go, then dashed across the street to a doorway in which three of his mates were standing.

'You won't believe this!' he said excitedly. 'Some big bloke's about to buy Vanish!'

Groan pushed open a rotted wooden gate to reveal a small yard containing a little old man and a very tired-looking black horse.

'Read the sign,' said Groan, padding up to the beast and examining it, carefully. 'He don't look that fast, though; he looks 'alf dead.'

'He costs fifty crowns,' said the old man, snappishly. 'That's fifty crowns; not forty and not sixty. Please yourself whether you buy him.'

Groan looked the horse over a few more times, then pulled its head up to face him.

'Looks like it's given up livin',' he said.

'Fifty crowns; please yourself.'

'One of its ears're 'anging off.'

'Don't buy him then.'

Groan cracked his knuckles.

'I'll give ya ten.'

The old man shrugged. 'Gate's behind you.'

'Twen'y.'

'Mind your step on the way out.'

'Furty.'

'Have a good walk.'

'Forty.'

'Nice day we're having.'

'Fortyfive.'

'Done.'

Groan counted out the money from his pouch, gave the old boy a couple of goblin teeth and made to walk the horse out of the yard.

'Hang on,' said the horse-seller, limping up to Groan and whispering in his ear. 'His name is Vanish, but you must NEVER say it aloud. Oh, and just to give you a bit of extra advice, the word that really makes him shift his speed is 'Loodafoodaroobakoobin,', but for goodness sake don't say *that* until you're well outside the town, or you'll end up with a broken neck for your trouble.'

'Say it 'gin; I didn' 'ear.'

The old man took another breath and whispered once more: 'Loodafoodaroobakoobin'.

'Nah, still dint get it.'

'Would you like me to write it down for you?'

'Nah, I can't read.'

The old man sighed.

'Yes, but you don't need to be able to read because you already know what the word is. I'm only writing it down so that you can *remember* it.'

'Yeah, all right.'

There was a few seconds of frantic scribbling on an old parchment.

'Here you go; don't lose it.'

Groan nodded, and lead the horse away.

The old man watched him go and gave a toothy grin.

CHAPTER
ELEVEN

'I didn't say a thing! I swear!'

Rorgrim Ripple shrank into the corner of the inn's back room as Effigy advanced on him.

'You better not have done, Ripple, or you'll have *me* and the rest of the boys to deal with and, just to remind you, that includes a vampire and one very big ogre.'

'D-do you think Burnie's dead?' Ripple ventured, straightening himself up as his attacker's expression began to soften.

'No, I don't,' Effigy replied. 'But no-one's heard from him yet and that's *never* a good sign.'

Rorgrim nodded. 'And he was called up to the palace, you say?'

'Along with two others, it would appear.'

'Well, whatever the reason, I'm telling you straight that I never said a thing about the group. Maybe Curfew just wanted to get rid of all the councillors?'

'Maybe,' Effigy conceded. 'But it's a pretty big coincidence, don't you think? What did they offer you; your own never-ending ale supply?'

'I didn't say anything. HONEST!'

'Hmm...well just make sure you *keep* saying nothing; that way, you have a half-chance of making it to your next birthday in one piece. Understood?'

'Yes; of course.'

'Right.' Effigy narrowed his eyes at the innkeeper one last time and departed.

HAVING LEFT Chudderford through the East Gate, Groan decided he would head for Wyka Bridge, the only authorised crossing point on the River Washin.

Peering behind him, he saw the town was still clearly visible: Vanish had hardly picked up the pace at all.

'C'mon,' Groan said, digging his heels into the beast's flank. 'Move it, will ya? I need ta get ta Dullitch.'

The horse slowed from a half-canter to a quarter-trot.

Groan rolled his eyes.

'Fooda-looda-roobi-cubon,' he said.

The horse came to a stop and craned to look back at him, pity in its eyes.

'Well?' Groan boomed. 'Move it!'

Nothing happened.

Groan climbed off the horse, said something utterly despicable about Gordo, and then tramped round to face it. Then, pulling the parchment from his belt, he said:

'Er...Looda-fooda-kooba-roobin?'

This time, the horse actually shook its head.

'Wha' is it, then?' Groan moaned. 'I don't wanna be stuck out 'ere f'rever.' He peered down at the parchment and back at the horse. Then he put one foot in the stirrups, swinging himself back atop the beast. 'I tell ya, I dunno *why* they call you Vanish.'

And, just like that, the horse showed him.

When Groan awoke, the clouds were skimming past at lightning speed and his granite head was hitting repeatedly off the bumpy ground. Every now and again, a hoof would come close to bludgeoning him into oblivion, and he felt the horse's flank smacking off his shoulder. He guessed what had happened before he managed to peer up: one of his feet had been caught in the stirrups.

'Hey!' he boomed at the insane horse. 'Stop, damn ya!'

But the only thing that had a decent chance of stopping Vanish was a crossbow bolt. The beast was galloping along like some kind of machine, its mind having evaporated somewhere in the fury of the flight.

Groan tried to reach for his sword, but he'd threaded it through the pack on the horse's opposite flank and now all he could see of it was the edge of the pommel.

He tried punching the beast a few times but Vanish's legs were pumping and its sides were like knotted rope.

Then he heard the cries:

'Hey you!'

'Halt!'

'Oi!'

'Drop the barrier!'

'Stop that horse!'

And the Wyka Bridge was suddenly left behind in a rain of splintering wood.

'Vanish!' Groan boomed. 'Vanish! Vanish! Vanish!'

And, sure enough, the horse accelerated. Threefold.

'Magic,' Groan muttered to himself, as he began to lose consciousness. 'Should've bloody known...'

~

'Effigy! Hey, Effigy!'

Jimmy Quickstint hurried through the marketplace and practically collided with his target.

'Sorry, but I – well – have you heard?'

'Have I heard *what*?' Effigy looked suddenly wretched, as if he knew what the thief was about to say even as he said it.

'Two councillors were found down by the harbour an hour ago, drowned.'

Effigy nodded.

'Do you know which two?'

'Yes,' said Jimmy, breathlessly. 'Taciturn Cadrick, the vice-chairman, and Rin Lye, the city's top judge.'

'The pair that were with Burnie at my hearing,' Effigy muttered. 'What's the official line?'

Jimmy sighed.

'They're saying that Viscount Curfew had dinner with the two of them and Burnie, before ordering Cadrick and Lye to travel over to Bulkas Island on council business; apparently, their boat capsized. Only, there's no sign of the boat and-'

'That's the biggest load of old rubbish I ever heard,' Effigy spat. 'Is that really all the palace could be bothered to come up with?'

'Yes; terrible, isn't it? They're saying that Burnie waited until his two colleagues were out of the way before making his attack on Curfew.'

'Laughable.'

'I'll say.' Jimmy whistled between his teeth. 'Should I send word to the others? I think we might need to meet up again.'

'Very well, but not until tonight: Shably is putting my plan into action and Nazz is still running his errand: he should return to Dullitch later this evening with some help.'

'OK; I'll go and tell Obegarde.'

'Good: and, remember, not a word to anybody. You never know who's listening in.'

'Understood. See you this evening.'

Effigy nodded and hurried away.

THE CART PROCEEDED along the dusty road to Dullitch, its varied occupants enjoying the fresh afternoon air.

'It's n-n-nice to get out once in a wh-while,' said Mifkindle, breathing deeply.

'Yeah, absolutely,' Victor agreed. 'We really don't do this enough, you and I: we should go for these travelling jobs more often.'

Mifkindle studied his friend for a second and then burst out laughing.

'What? What did I say that was funny?'

'Well, let's f-face it, Vic. You *had* to g-get away, didn't you?'

'Oh?' said Nazz, leaning across Gordo with a grin only an ogre could muster. 'What did you do then? Something terrible? C'mon, spill the beans.'

He and Gordo looked at the young assassin expectantly, but it was Mifkindle who spoke first.

'Vic k-killed his f-f-form tutor,' he said, in a matter-of-fact voice.

Nazz nodded. 'And I'm right in thinking that's bad, am I?'

'Not in itself,' Victor admitted. 'But the school we both went to has a strange rule: when a pupil passes all his exams, he has to take on his form tutor in a game that's sort of like cat and mouse. Only, ours got out of control because I accidentally pushed him off a church roof-'

'Accidentally, n-n-notice-' Mifkindle grinned.

'-yeah, and so Rumlink Banks-'

'That's the t-teacher-'

'-made it a fight to the death. I won, but the school staff were really annoyed at losing their most feared teacher...so they raised him from the grave.'

'Ah...' said Gordo, sharing an amused glance with Nazz. 'And I take it he came back mad?'

'He came back insane and undead,' Victor shivered at the thought. 'Then he killed half the teachers on the staff and came after me: I managed to give him the slip on a rooftop on the outskirts of Legrash, but he swore that he'd hunt me down until the end of time.'

'Nice,' said Nazz, flicking the reigns a little. 'It's always good to have teachers you can get on with. Hahaha!'

All four of the travellers erupted into fits of laughter, until Nazz's expression changed. The big ogre was peering into the distance.

'What in the name of-'

Gordo saw it, too: an immense cloud of dust rising from something that was heading, inexorably, towards them.

'What do think it is?' Victor asked. 'A spell of some kind?'

Nazz shook his head. 'Not coming from that direction. North-wise, there's not a civilized town between here and the Washin. Whatever it is, it's either come over the Wyka Bridge or from the river itself. Look at it go!'

'Aren't we in the way?' Victor hazarded, noting that Nazz wasn't exactly rushing to move the cart.

'No,' said the ogre, dismissively. 'By the look of things, that dust-ball is on a straight course for Dullitch.'

'It's not a b-b-ball,' said Mifkindle, who'd produced a spyglass and was peering carefully into it. 'It's a rider-less horse.'

'Seriously?' Victor whistled between his teeth. 'It's really going some, isn't it?'

'Fastest horse I ever saw,' Nazz confessed. 'Must be enchanted or something.'

Gordo agreed. 'And it's rider-less, you say?'

'I t-t-tell a lie,' said Mifkindle, turning the base of the spyglass. 'There *is* a rider, b-b-but he's hanging off on the f-far side. D-damn, that chap must be in p-p-pain.'

Gordo rolled his eyes.

'It's not a big fella by any chance, is it?' he asked.

'Hmm...looks like a giant.'

'It's Groan Teethgrit,' said the dwarf, with a sigh. 'Don't ask me how I know; I just *know*.'

Mifkindle started to pack the spyglass away. 'W-well,' he said. 'Whoever it is, they're g-going to reach the c-c-city long before us.'

Nazz took the reigns up and moved the horses on once more.

'We're not actually heading straight into the city,' he explained.

'No?' said Victor.

'We're n-not?' Mifkindle added.

'Nope. We're going to take the cart *close* to the North

Gate. Then, just before we reach it, we're going to veer right and follow the city wall until we get to the South Sea. Hopefully, there will be a boat waiting to take us into Dullitch Harbour.'

'In that case, you can drop us at the gate,' said Gordo. 'We've no city passes, but we don't usually have any trouble getting in.'

'Ha! I'll bet.'

'Thanks a lot for the lift, Nazz; it was good to meet you.'

The ogre nodded.

'And you,' he said. 'Go careful.'

CHAPTER
TWELVE

The scribe hurried into the throne room of Dullitch Palace, bowed low, and unfurled a scroll.

'Excellency,' he began. 'I spoke to the Rooftop Runners about the list of assassins you wanted.'

Diveal yawned. 'And?'

'And they're sorry to report that they don't have any available members in the city who would suit the role of royal bodyguard. They were quite unhelpful, actually...and several of them laughed at me. The masters were even so rude as to suggest an undead member who's causing a great deal of havoc up in Legrash: I told them they could stuff-'

'An undead assassin,' Diveal interrupted. 'Powerful, is he?'

The scribe swallowed a few times and nodded.

'A veritable "machine of murder" according to the Rooftop's Legrasian associate.'

'Perfect: have him contained, boxed up and shipped down here.'

'Y-you actually want to employ him?'

'Of course; he'll be perfect.'

'V-very well, Excellency. I shall contact them at once. However, there will be the small matter of-'

'Pay them whatever they ask for: it'll be worth it if I can control him...'

The scribe pursed his lips.

'I'm afraid there's little chance of *that*, Excellency. The creature is said to be bestial and beyond the will of any man. You'd need to have powers of mind control to-'

'That will be all.'

As the scribe bowed once more and scuttled out, Vortas Lythay emerged from a shadowy corner of the room.

'An undead assassin, master?' he said, biting his bottom lip and breathing deeply. 'Wouldn't it be a little unwise of Viscount Curfew to have one of those running around the palace?'

Diveal shrugged.

'It's not unwise if you possess the power of mind control,' he said.

'And do you have that power, master?' asked Vortas, one eyebrow raised.

'Of course I do; I am a man of many...talents. Besides, if things take a turn for the worst, I can always kill it.'

'Kill an assassin, master?'

'Absolutely; assassins are not all they're rumoured to be.' He cracked his knuckles. 'Now bring me some food...and remember *not* to poison it.'

By the time Vanish arrived, in a great swath of dust, the two guards on sentry duty at Dullitch's North Gate had already called for backup and were preparing to repel a full-scale attack.

Therefore, they were all incredibly surprised when a lone horse came trotting out of the swirl, dragging a semi-conscious figure behind it.

Abruptly, it stopped.

'Where am I?' said Groan, hazily.

One of the guards knelt beside him, as others arrived.

'Dullitch,' he said, leaning on the base of his pike. 'North Gate; looks like you've got horse trouble.' He turned back to his colleagues, several of whom looked suddenly in awe.

'That's the king of Phlegm!' said one. 'That's Groan Teethgrit.'

'He's right!' said another. 'I'd recognise him anywhere.'

'S'me,' Groan confirmed. 'Now get out o' me way so I can stan' up.'

They stood back and watched the giant barbarian unfold, upwards: a fully stretched Groan was quite a sight to behold, and only the horse looked unimpressed. That is, until Groan reeled back and punched it in the side of the head.

Vanish whinnied a little, but stood its ground.

'I curse ya, ya damn fing,' Groan boomed. 'Ya can rot in 'ell.'

'Are you here on official business, Your Majesty?' said the first guard, trying to change the subject. 'Should we notify the viscount of your arrival?'

'Nah,' said Groan, sniffing. 'Listen; have 'ny dwarfs come fru 'ere, las' coupla days?'

The two guards at the front of the unit shared a glance, then one took out a scroll and consulted it, carefully.

'Hmm...43 dwarfs, Your Majesty. Can you be a little more specific?'

Groan frowned. 'Eh?'

'Can you tell us anything that might single the dwarf you're looking for out of the crowd?' explained another.

'Er...yeah. He'd be draggin' a corpse wiv 'im; only, the bloke ain't dead, he's jus' sleepin'. 'Sme bruvver.'

There was a moment of confusion before one of the guards managed to grasp at a straw.

'Is the dwarf from Phlegm?'

'Yeah. S'right.'

'Then the answer's no, I'm afraid. No Phlegm-issued passes have gone through the gates this week.'

Groan nodded. 'Then I'm gonna wait 'ere,' he said, leaning against the wall.

The two sentry guards nodded and returned to their posts. The rest filtered back into the city proper.

After a moment's silence, one of the pair said: 'My name's Tom, by the way, and I'm very pleased to meet you. Your name is legend in this city.'

'Yeah; 's cause I'm 'ard,' said Groan. ''ere, Tom; d'you wanna buy an 'orse?'

~

NAZZ REIGNED IN THE HORSES, causing the cart to come to a rocking halt.

'Is here all right for you?' he asked, gesturing to the side of the road. 'Sorry, but I probably can't get any closer to the North Gate without being seen.'

'That's fine,' said Gordo, gratefully. 'If you can just help me down with Gape, I can drag him the rest of the way.'

Nazz climbed off the side of the cart and together, they lowered the big barbarian onto the grass.

'Nice to meet you all,' said Gordo, patting Nazz on the arm and mock saluting the assassins. 'It's been...interesting.'

'It certainly has,' Victor agreed.

'Hope to b-b-bump into you a-g-gain,' added Mifkindle.

Nazz returned to his seat at the front of the cart and urged the horses onward.

'Right,' said Gordo, watching him go. 'Let's see if we can get you some help, eh?' He grabbed hold of Gape's boots and began to drag the warrior towards Dullitch.

A little over an hour later, he drew close to the North Gate, and saw a recognisable form leaning against the wall beside the portcullis.

'You took ya' time,' Groan said, padding over to him. 'I bin 'ere *ages*.'

Gordo muttered something under his breath, then noticed that his friend was limping.

'Fall off a horse did you?' he enquired.

The giant barbarian nodded. 'Yeah; the 'orse I bought bolted an' I got knocked out.'

'I thought as much; reckon I saw you having trouble earlier this afternoon. I can't be sure though; I was so relaxed in the *coach* I hitched a ride on, I might've dreamed it.'

'Yer coach can't 'ave bin that great,' said Groan, doggedly. 'Seein' as I still beat you 'ere...in me sleep.'

'All right! Fine! You win; *again*. Now, are you going to help me with Gape or do I have to drag him through the gates by myself?'

Groan reached down and heaved his brother over one shoulder.

'Right,' he boomed. 'You still got the 'ammer.'

Gordo nodded. 'Of course I have: it's right here.'

'Good: we can go an' see Curfew 'fore we look for a room.'

'Don't you think we should get Gape sorted out first?' Gordo exclaimed. 'We can always trade the hammer in the morning!'

'I wanna do it now.'

'In the morning!'

'Now.'

'IN THE MORNING.'

Groan scratched his chin. 'I'm the King of Phlegm,' he boomed. 'An' I say we do the trade fing now.'

'Right,' said Gordo. 'And I'm the dwarf who's telling you you can't have the hammer until tomorrow morning.'

'I found it!'

'And I told you where to look, you ungrateful idiot! I spent months in the library researching legends: and do I get any thanks? Do I hell! You – you – you great big lummox!'

'Yeah? Least I ain't two foot tall.'

'I'm four foot one!'

'Oh, go an' stuff y'self.'

'AFTER YOU.'

The two mercenaries glared at each other for a moment.

'Open up,' Groan warned the sentry. ''S King Groan...an' 'is dwarf.'

Gordo swore quietly as the portcullis was raised.

Two guards were blocking the path. 'We do recognise you, Your Majesty, but we're still going to need to see some identification from the dwarf and, um, the sleeping gentleman. Do you have a city pass, Master Dwarf?'

'I'm here on business,' Gordo growled. 'And, as a matter of fact, you're addressing the Supreme Guard Captain of

Phlegm...and this, here, is the King's brother. Now get out of my way or die!'

'Yeah,' said Groan, drawing his broadsword. 'Wan' a mouthful o' cold steel?'

The guards smiled at one another nervously.

'PASS!' they said, in unison.

CHAPTER
THIRTEEN

'Lice! Eugh! Who's given me head-lice?'

Brigadier Lanslide shook his comb free of the mites and glared around the room.

'Don't look at me, sir,' said Colonel Reish. 'The ruddy things are crawling all over *my* comb, too. Maybe one of the privates brought us some dirty washing water or something?'

'Dirty is right,' said the brigadier, momentarily disgusted by the contents of his own head. 'Never thought I'd live to see the day when anything got into my lovely locks.

The other officer looked at him; it *was* quite incredible to find lice on a bald man.

'It's possible they came from your chest hair, sir,' Colonel Reish advised. 'I mean, you do hear of such creatures migrating north for the winter.'

'What, you mean they're chest lice? Oh, surely there's no such thing!'

'Excuse me, sirs, but I couldn't help overhearing.'

The two officers turned as Senior Guard Shably marched

into the room, carrying a pair of scissors and a bowl of what looked like steaming water.

'There *has* been a minor outbreak of lice in the palace, this week. I've already treated some of the men; I'd be only too pleased to help...'

'What sort of treatment?' asked the Colonel, apparently horrified at the sight of water.

Shably smiled.

'I'm really glad you asked, sirs. This treatment basically requires me to cover a tiny section of your hair with my special solution. Then, all the lice hurry to the section of hair containing the solution, as it contains certain, er, properties that the little demons cannot resist, and I cut off the offending section of hair, ending the lice problem indefinitely.'

Brigadier Lanslide marched over to Shably and peered into the bowl.

'Looks like hot, soapy water to me,' he said.

'Aye, that is it, sir,' Shably conceded. 'But, to the lice, it's like a...er...acid, sir.'

Night had already stretched its icy fingers over Dullitch by the time a small rowing boat appeared at the harbour gates. Fortunately, the watchtowers were being manned by imbeciles, so Obegarde had no trouble manoeuvring the little boat beneath them. Keeping close to the outside of the city walls, he drew towards the bank, where a cart was waiting.

Nazz jumped down from his seat and hurried into the water to help the vampire haul in the boat.

'Got a pair of worthy passengers for you, sir,' he said, in a derisory tone.

'Very kind of you,' said Obegarde, with equally false aplomb. 'Do hope I can speed them into the city as fast as you brought them here!'

'I do not doubt that you will.'

The boat settled, Nazz turned to face his two companions and beckoned them forward. Victor and Mifkindle both hurried into the boat.

'Good luck,' the ogre whispered, before hurrying back to his cart and turning it toward the city's North Gate.

'Welcome to Dullitch,' Obegarde said, shaking each of the assassins firmly by the hand. 'I'm Jareth Obegarde, your boatman for this evening: I'm taking you to meet with Effigy Spatula.'

'That's a b-b-big relief,' said Mifkindle.

'Yeah,' added Victor. 'We're not used to all this cloak and dagger stuff.'

'Not used to it? But you're assassins! You must have to do this sort of thing all the time! You know, hiding in the shadows and so forth...'

'Not really,' Victor whispered, ducking as a guard leaned over the nearest watchtower. 'And certainly not in a boat.'

'I tend to get s-s-seasick,' Mifkindle admitted, leaning over the side of the boat for reasons of his own. 'Can we j-just stop t-t-talking and get into the c-c-city.'

Obegarde nodded and reached for the oars.

'Sure thing,' he said. 'Hold on tight: if we get seen here, we're in deep trouble.'

∼

Effigy Spatula stood on the edge of the longest pier in Dullitch Harbour and shook his head gravely.

'It's going to be too close,' he said, watching the guard towers. 'The guards are having a changeover and the new lot look a good deal more awake.' He turned to Jimmy Quickstint. 'We *have* to create a diversion; if Obegarde is found sneaking two assassins into the city, he'll be dragged before Curfew...and after what happened with Burnie, we absolutely *cannot* take any chances.'

Jimmy squinted at the nearest tower. 'I can probably create a decent diversion for one tower, but what about the other?'

'We need to get both, ideally,' said Effigy, rubbing his chin. 'And we need to discuss phase three of the plan.'

'Phase three?' Jimmy exclaimed. 'What happened to the first two?'

Effigy sighed. 'Phase one is underway, and phase two involves the friends I have coming in on the boat. Now, what are you going to do to distract the watchtower guards? Come on: we've only got a few moments!'

Jimmy glanced back at the harbour scene, a bead of sweat forming on his forehead.

'I'm going to start a fire,' he said, running off towards the nearest tower.

Effigy gawped after him.

'You're what? I meant a *small* diversion; A SMALL ONE!'

But Jimmy was already a dot in the distance.

~

'Steady,' Obegarde warned, pulling in the oars and holding the boat still for a moment. '*These* guards are doing regular sweeps; they must have changed shifts. Stay DOWN!'

'I am d-d-down,' said Mifkindle, who was still being sick. 'I couldn't be any more d-down if I was clinically d-d-depressed.'

'Shhh!'

Victor, who was practically crouched flat in the middle of the boat, muttered something under his breath and suddenly let loose an arm. Obegarde, sitting next to him, saw a flash of movement and then heard a splash.

'What the hell was that?'

'A guard,' Victor explained. 'I just got one with a pebble.'

'You what?'

'I just knocked out a guard with a pebble; luckily, he fell into the water and-'

'You idiot! You absolute moron! They'll all have heard the splash! We'll be surrounded in seconds!'

Sure enough, a group of guards had gathered at the top of the watchtower to look for their fallen comrade.

'How the hell did you get to become an assassin with ideas like that?' Obegarde whispered. 'Did you inherit the job?'

'I'm sorry!' Victor snapped back. 'I didn't think.'

'No, Vic,' Mifkindle added. 'You never d-d-do.'

'Hang about,' Obegarde interrupted, staring up at the tower-top. 'Something's happening! They're all going away.'

'Yeah,' Mifkindle observed. 'They're p-probably coming d-d-down here to get a closer l-l-look.'

'You're right.'

Obegarde nodded and began to row as he'd never rowed before.

'FIRE! FIRE!'

Guards ran in every direction as the windows at the base of the west tower exploded.

Effigy concealed a smile as he watched the darting form of Jimmy Quickstint hurry from the shadows of the first tower, across the harbour, to the shadows of the other.

There came the sound of breaking glass before the east tower, too, was alight.

'Fire! FIRE!'

The cry was infectious, and it was spreading. Several citizens arrived with buckets drawn from the ocean and a group outside the Crushload Inn had inexplicably started a chain that consisted of ale tankards: it didn't seem to be moving very fast, though.

'Ale does wonders for fire,' a drinker explained to Effigy when he saw him looking in bewilderment at the group. 'Er...honest.'

Jimmy arrived, skidding to a halt, beside the freedom fighter, where he promptly collapsed.

'Well done,' Effigy whispered. 'Splendid work, in fact; you've got the whole place in an uproar.'

The thief wiped some sweat from the corners of his eyes and pointed across at the harbour wall.

'There they are,' he said weakly.

'Fantastic! Look; nobody's even paying attention! You did a first-class job there, Jimmy boy. First-class!'

Jimmy peered up at the freedom fighter.

'No problem,' he muttered. 'Causing trouble is the only thing I'm any good at.'

GROAN AND GORDO marched through the streets of Dullitch, Gape slung haphazardly over his brother's shoulder.

'How about down here?' the dwarf suggested, pointing toward a street that was labelled 'Candleford Row'. 'Looks as good as any other...'

Groan nodded. 'Yeah, s'pose.'

They proceeded down the street, stopping intermittently at shops that looked like they might contain healing potions of one sort or another.

'This one sells candles,' Gordo said, stopping at the window of a small and rather ramshackle building. 'Maybe he can sniff himself better.'

Groan shrugged and lowered Gape to the cobbles.

'Wurf a try, innit?'

'Agreed. Pity it's shut, really. Maybe we can come back in the morn-GROAN!'

Gordo watched in frank astonishment as Groan swung back a leg, kicked the front door open and strode inside the shop, emerging a few seconds later with two candles.

'How do we light 'em?'

'We don't!' Gordo screamed. 'We get arrested for breaking and entering, you dim-witted ape!'

The owner of the candle shop, an elderly woman with her hair concealed behind a topaz bed-cap, came hurtling out of the doorway, waving what looked like a snub-nosed mace.

'Take this, you thieving scum!' she cried, laying six blows on Groan's chest before he could even think to raise his hand in defence.

'GOLD!' Gordo yelled, thinking on his feet. 'We're fully

prepared to pay you twenty GOLD for any candle that helps our friend here.'

The old woman stopped her assault on the giant barbarian before glancing down at Gordo.

'He broke into my shop!'

'No, he didn't.' The dwarf shook his head. 'Actually, he *fell* into your shop; he's really clumsy.'

The old woman peered back at her broken door. 'Twenty gold, you say? And what about the damage to my door?'

'Make it thirty,' Gordo offered, reaching inside his armour for the trusty money pouch he always kept there.

'Done!' said the old woman, when she heard the clink of coins. 'Now, what's wrong with your friend?'

Groan shrugged. 'He smashed up one o' them glass balls.'

'I wasn't asking *you*, Butterfoot! I was asking your dwarf friend.'

'We don't know,' Gordo admitted. 'But he *did* break an enchanted sphere of some sort; and just before he passed out, he was screaming like a newborn baby.'

'Ah,' said the old woman, knowingly. 'One of *that* sort, then: I've got just the candle for you. Follow me...'

She disappeared inside the building, and Groan wandered in after her. Gordo sighed deeply and, with a little effort, managed to drag Gape into the shop.

'Here you go,' she said, running her finger along the top of a dusty shelf and plucking a purple candle from the dozen or so lined up there. 'This'll have your friend on his feet in no time, but it'll take a lot of effort on your behalf.'

'Us?' Groan boomed. 'Wha' do we 'ave ta do?'

The old woman limped over to the front door, closed and locked it.

'Well,' she said, carefully. 'The candle will do some of the work, but the rest is done by concentration; and that, of course, requires effort.'

'Er...'

'No problem,' Gordo cut in, before his partner could complain. 'It's VERY nice of you to help us. Isn't it, Groan?'

'I s'pose.'

'Exactly. So, madam, where do you want us to put Gape while we're concentrating?'

The old woman cleared a bench of some strange-looking rubble and indicated that the duo should lay their fallen comrade there.

'Make sure he's put in a relaxed position,' she advised, fixing the candle on a plate and pulling two chairs up to the bench. She watched as Groan and Gordo lifted Gape gently onto the rough wooden surface. 'That's it; that's perfect. OK, now you each need to take one of the chairs by his feet while I light the candle...ready?'

'Yes.'

'Yeah.'

'OK.' The old woman lit the candle, which immediately gave off a very peculiar smell. 'Now, stare into the candle and repeat after me: Bolin Ritesh Kamara.'

'Bolin Ritesh Kamara,' said Groan, repeating the words with such accuracy that Gordo almost fainted through shock.

'Bolin Ritesh Kamara,' he echoed.

'Excellent,' the old woman finished. 'That brings us to the end of the procedure.'

'That's it?' Gordo exclaimed. 'But he's still asleep!'

'Yes, I know.'

'So what happens now, then?'

'Well,' the old woman smiled. 'Now you'll do whatever I want you to do…and I want you to tie yourselves up.'

'Welcome to the headquarters of the Secret Army,' said Effigy Spatula, leading the two assassins into the back room of the Crushload Inn. 'I'm afraid the mood in here is sombre because we've just learned that our chairman has been lost to the enemy.' He turned on his heels as he spoke. 'I am sorry about your difficult journey, gentlemen; I assure you that things will be very straightforward from here on in.'

Victor and Mifkindle took their seats at the table, while Obegarde and Jimmy gathered around them like royalists at a coronation.

'I'd like to introduce you all to Mifkindle Green and Victor Franklin, expert assassins,' Effigy went on. 'These are my co-conspirators; Jimmy Quickstint and the man who ferried you in, Jareth Obegarde. You've met Nazz, of course; I'm assuming he'll be along here just as soon as he's parked the cart – and Shably, our final member, is also due back in the next ten minutes.'

'What exactly are these two doing here?' Obegarde asked, expectantly.

Effigy smiled.

'I'm fully intending to tell you just as soon as Nazz and Shably arrive; I don't want to have to explain the plan twice.'

Fortunately, he didn't need to, as both Nazz and Shably chose that moment to enter the room.

'Evening,' said the ogre, crashing down into one of the free chairs and putting both hands behind his head. 'Poor

Burnie; I'm really going to miss him. When I get my hands on that scumbag impostor-'

Effigy smiled.

'I have news of Burnie,' he said.

Every eye at the table turned towards the freedom fighter, who was holding aloft a rolled parchment.

'Our dubious friend Rorgrim Ripple received this a few hours ago, by ravensage. I don't know where it came from, but it says: "The Secret Army has a friend who must hide. Nevertheless, he is safe, and already a good distance from here. The fight must be continued, and won. B."'

There was a new silence around the table, but it was a silence born of determination.

'I've already sent a message back by the same bird, telling Burnie all of my plans and assuring him of our intentions to see them through.'

There were several murmurs of agreement.

'Now, Mr Shably,' said Effigy slowly, setting a flame to the parchment. 'Do you have any encouraging results for us?'

Shably didn't say anything. He merely walked around the group and deposited two packets of hair on the tabletop, grinning proudly at his handiwork.

'Ha! I had every faith in you!' Effigy said. 'Now, if everyone takes a seat, I can begin to outline the first two phases of my grand scheme.'

Chairs were gathered and several candles extinguished as silence descended on the little room.

'Right,' said Effigy, after a time. 'Thanks to Mr Shably, we can now make our move. Tomorrow evening, we will walk into the palace disguised as two of its most senior officers. Senior officers, I might add, who will themselves have been incapacitated by our good friend, Nazz. Once safely inside, we will head for the throne room and confront Viscount Curfew over his true identity.'

Several looks of surprise greeted him.

'That's it?' Jimmy exclaimed, leaning back in his chair with a very disappointed look on his face. 'That's your grand plan? He'll have us executed in five seconds flat!'

Effigy shook his head.

'No, he won't be able to do that, because a) he won't know who we really are and b) we'll have the protection of two master assassins and an ogre who will be escorted into the palace as our prisoners.'

'OK,' said Obegarde, evenly. 'But say everything goes well, and we confront Curfew; what happens then? Even if we *do* get away, we'll have achieved nothing aside from getting two senior officers executed as a result of our own stupidity!'

Effigy folded his arms and swore under his breath.

'Do you have any better suggestions?' he snapped.

It was Jimmy who answered. 'As a matter of fact I do.'

'Well, I'm sure we'd all love to hear them, master thief.'

'Fine. I suggest that we plant a barrel of fumeback powder in the secret tunnel beside Curfew's room and detonate it. Beforehand, we could cause a diversion to get most of the guards out of that side of the palace, and-'

'Oh, really?' Effigy shook his head. 'And that's a sensible plan, is it?'

'Well, I think it's-'

'You propose to do this without knowing for sure if the man on the throne of Dullitch is, in fact, an impostor?'

Jimmy jumped to his feet. 'Ha! How does *your* plan inflict any less damage? In actual fact, how does *your* plan achieve anything at all? It's utterly ridiculous.'

'Er...excuse us,' said Victor. 'But, and I really don't mean to be rude, we've come to Dullitch to do a job...and if you lot don't stop arguing, we're going to start right here.'

'S-s-seconded,' said Mifkindle, humourlessly.

Nazz suddenly got out of his chair and laid both his ham-sized hands on the tabletop.

'Why don't we start with Effigy's plan and, if that fails, move on to Jimmy's one. We have to do *something* because Burnie was my friend and I don't reckon he would *ever* have raised a hand against the *real* viscount.'

'No,' Effigy said. 'I agree...and that's why we have to put ALL parts of the plan into action at once.'

'What was that?'

'Eh?'

'You can't be serious!'

'I am,' Effigy assured them. 'You will infiltrate the palace, unmask the viscount and attempt to reason with him...while I will ensure that, if reason fails, we have fumeback powder to resort to.'

'You're going to do it?' Nazz exclaimed. 'You're actually going to sneak into the palace with a barrel full of Fumeback powder, find the secret door to the even more secret tunnel, wait to see whether our part of the plan fails, then plant and detonate the charge...ALL BY YOURSELF? That's madness!'

'I know,' said Effigy, with a smile. 'But doing mad and insufferably stupid things is what freedom is all about: in the end.'

'Hmm...excuse me?' said Shably quietly.

Effigy turned to him with surprise: he'd forgotten the guard was still there. 'Yes?'

'Is that all you'll be wanting me for? Only, you said that I wouldn't be needed after tonight...'

'And I meant it. Your work here is complete...'

Shably turned to leave.

'...almost.'

The guard released a heavy sigh but remained in the doorway. 'What *else* can I do, Mr Spatula?'

Effigy scribbled something on a scrap of parchment, then hurried across the room and handed it to the guard. 'You can set off the palace fire bell at *this* time on the morning of our infiltration.'

Shably snatched the parchment, read it and nodded.

'Good man,' said Effigy, patting the guard on the shoulder. 'Undoubtedly the best of us all.'

'I DON'T BELIEVE THIS,' said Gordo, miserably, yanking at the ropes that bound him to his friend. 'I really, really don't.'

Groan made a few vague sounds, but he was still semi-conscious.

'We should have known she wouldn't help after we kicked down her door!' Gordon snapped. 'Do the candle trick to make your friend better, my foot! Now we're stuck in her cellar – only the gods know how she got us down here – and she's taken all our gold! Oh, and you can be damn sure she's gone straight to the city guard. We'll be dragged before Curfew like petty thieves; and how embarrassing is that for the King of Phlegm? I tell you, why we don't see these things coming is anybody's guess!'

'Eh?' Groan muttered, 'Who said that? Where am I?'

'Oh, joy! He's awake! Welcome back to the world of the living, oat-brain.'

'What 'appened? Did Gape wake up?'

'Hmm...before we get onto the subject of Gape, let me answer your first question. The old woman whose shop you BROKE INTO tricked us. She made us sniff the funny candles - which put us to sleep - then she roped us up in her basement and went to fetch the guards. Now, on a scale of one to ten, how dumb do you feel? Because I'm feeling pretty stupid down here, I can tell you.'

Groan thought for a moment.

'Yeah,' he said. 'But did Gape wake up?'

'NO! SHE WAS LYING! HE'S PROBABLY STILL UPSTAIRS ON THE BENCH!'

'Oh, right. 'Cause I broke her door, you reckon?'

'YES!'

The big barbarian nodded. 'Good trick, weren' it? Stitchin' us up wiv candles an' all 'at?'

'Yes, Groan. It was a very good trick, and we both fell for it.'

'So 'ow do we get out of 'ere?'

Gordo shook his head.

'I've absolutely no idea. I don't know about you, but I'm tied up tighter than Muttknuckles' wallet.'

'Yeah, me too. Don't reckon I can get out wivout breakin' an arm: I still feel really weak from the candle sniffin'.'

'I don't think you'll need to,' Gordo advised him, peering up at the cellar roof. 'I can hear guards; lots of them, and they sound like they're heading this way.'

There was a series of trampling footsteps overhead, and then candlelight streamed into the basement.

The old woman appeared, followed by a senior-looking guard and several others.

'That's them,' she said, holding the candle over the

dynamic duo. 'Broke into my shop, they did. The other one's upstairs, asleep.'

'The one on the bench?'

'Yes.'

'Is he still alive?' Gordo hazarded and got a clip round the ear for his trouble.

'Thank you, madam,' said the guard. 'We'll take it from here.' He leaned over Groan.

'Name?'

'Stuff off.'

'I'll ask again. Name?'

'His name's Groan Teethgrit,' Gordo muttered.

'Groan Teethgrit,' the guard repeated. 'That name sounds familiar. What's your current occupation, Mr Teethgrit?'

Groan peered up at him. 'I'm a sheppad.'

'He's the reigning King of Phlegm,' Gordo interrupted. 'Don't you recognise him? It's THE Groan Teethgrit: there's only one.'

The guard crouched down beside Groan and raised his lamp.

'Great gods, so it is!' he said. 'Right lads: I think we've got one for Lord Curfew, here.' He put his head on one side and studied the ropes. 'Haul 'em away, but don't untie these knots; they look...solid.'

'They *are*,' said the old woman, proudly.

The guard nodded. 'Good work, ma'am: you can leave them to us now... and I'll send some boys upstairs for the other intruder. C'mon: let's move out!'

'THIS IS the first and most important part of the plan,' said Effigy, leaning in towards Nazz and lowering his voice to a conspiratorial whisper. The others were all listening intently. 'Tomorrow morning, after the daily parade, the most senior officers in Dullitch will do as they always do and have breakfast together. These officers, who you will recognise from Shably's descriptions, will include our two good friends, Colonel Reish and Brigadier Lanslide, as well as the general himself. It is during this feast that Nazz and our two assassins are going to enter the courtyard and kidnap them.'

'We're what?' said Nazz. 'With fifty guards on duty? We won't stand a chance!'

'On the contrary,' Effigy advised. 'It will be quite easy. I've watched the parade for a few days now, and it has a certain monotonous routine to it. The soldiers all disperse after a few marches, leaving the senior officers to socialise in a tent on the left of the courtyard gate. Now, if my guess is correct, they will have two outlined priorities during any disturbance: the palace and the general. Any lower ranks will only be worried about *afterwards*. So, if attacked by *experts* and a creature of your – forgive my description – ferocity, they will send for backup before attacking...and by the time that arrives you will be back on the streets with two unconscious officers in your cart.'

The ogre nodded.

'So, basically, all we have to do is ambush the remnants of the parade, crash into the big tent on the left, knock the two officers spark out and take them to you lot...who will be waiting where?'

'We'll be in the back yard of the corner house on Oval Square, so you won't have far to ride in the confusion. We'll already be transformed into our officer shapes because we're going to drop the hairs into our dust in a few seconds: each pouch should last forty-eight hours.'

'Right,' said Nazz, gulping back his trepidation. 'Then what?'

Effigy grinned.

'Then we tie the officers up, clap you, Mifkindle and Victor in irons and return to the palace as heroes! Champion officers! Men of metal!'

'And what happens when we get inside the palace?' Jimmy asked, with Obegarde nodding behind him.

'Ah,' Efiggy allowed himself a theatrical deep breath. 'Then, I'm afraid we wing it,' he finished.

CHAPTER
FOURTEEN

It was approaching midnight in Dullitch, and the palace was almost in total darkness.

The guard on duty outside Viscount Curfew's bedroom was characteristically asleep at his post, so the herald decided not to bother waking him and knocked on the door instead.

The guard didn't wake up, but neither, it seemed, did the viscount.

The herald rapped louder.

Still nothing.

'W-what's happening?' said the guard, suddenly roused by the noise. 'Where am I?'

'On duty,' said the herald. 'Supposedly.'

'Are you after the viscount?'

'Yes.'

'Oh.' The guard struggled lazily to his feet. 'Well, the viscount is in the North Tower, and he gave orders that he isn't to be disturbed under any circumstances.'

'You can tell-'

'WHATSOEVER.'

'OK, fine.' The herald nodded. 'But I have the King of Phlegm downstairs...as a prisoner. What am I supposed to do about that?'

The guard stroked his beard. 'Well, Lord Curfew said that if there was an emergency, you could call on his new chief of staff to deal with it.'

'His new chief of staff?' The herald frowned. 'Since when?'

'This afternoon: his private quarters are at the end of this corridor, on the right.'

The herald nodded, and dashed along the corridor, skidding to a halt outside a door with a plaque that read:

VORTAS LYTHAY

PALACE ADMINISTRATOR

He raised a hand to knock, but the door opened before he could touch it.

'Good evening,' said Vortas, only his pale face outlined in the candlelight. 'What can I do for you?'

The herald swallowed.

'Um...it's King Teethgrit, sir, of Phlegm. He's been brought in as a prisoner, sir, because he burgled a shop in-'

'Very well.' Vortas muttered. 'Have him brought into the throne room; I will see him there.'

'He says he wants to see Viscount Curfew or they'll be trouble, sir...'

'You have my orders.'

'Yes, sir. I'll see to it right away, sir.' The herald turned to leave, then had another thought and peered back at the administrator. 'Oh, one other thing, si-'

'Yes?'

'He's got another two fellows with him; it seems that one's his brother – a few problems there - and the other is the Captain of the Phlegmian Guard. And what with Phlegm being the richest kingdom in Illmoor, I wasn't sure if we should-'

'Of course.' Vortas took a deep breath. 'Treat them all as guests, but only admit the king to the throne room.'

'Very well, sir: he's restrained at the moment. Should we untie him?'

'No. But go now; don't keep him waiting...and have some scrolls sent up to me: I want to look as official as possible when I make my entrance...'

'Yes, sir; I'll see to it at once. And...'

'And?' Vortas gasped. 'You mean there's something ELSE?'

'Y-yes, sir. The...er...*thing* that Lord Curfew ordered has arrived, sir.'

'Really? That was quick!'

'Y-yes, sir. It seems the Legrasians couldn't wait to get rid of it, so they flew it down on the back of a Garji.

'I see. Have it taken to the viscount's office immediately...and move yourself: I don't want the king of Phlegm kept waiting!'

'Yes, sir!'

'And remember the scrolls!'

'Yes, sir!'

The herald nodded, turned and hared off down the corridor.

'Give us me sword back,' said Groan, stomping into the throne room like a child whose favourite toy had been confiscated. 'An' get these ropes off 'fore I brain ya.'

The guards managed to coax the giant barbarian into the largest of the easy chairs and turned him to face the throne. It was at this moment that the herald arrived, his face red with the effort of running.

'Where's Curfew?' Groan boomed.

The herald bowed before him.

'His Excellency is otherwise engaged, Your Majesty. He is therefore dispatching his most senior aide to assist you during this difficult time.'

Groan fought against his bonds, but the old woman's complicated knots were lethal. In the end, he gave up the struggle.

'Who 'm I seein' 'stead, then?' he demanded.

'You will be received by Mr Lythay, the palace administrator.'

'Who? I never 'eard of 'im.'

'Yes, well, Mr Lythay is very new to the job, but I can assure you-'

'-that you will be treated with the utmost respect, Your Majesty!' Vortas finished, striding into the throne room with a handful of scrolls. 'Get those ropes off him immediately; that man is the KING OF PHLEGM!'

The herald, a little confused by the sudden turnaround, snapped his fingers and the guards set to work on the knots.

'Would you like a drink, Your Majesty?' Lythay continued in his falsely obsequious tone. 'An ale, perhaps? Or something more refined; how do you take your wine?'

Groan sniffed.

'I'll 'ave an ale, cheers.'

'Of course.' Vortas turned to the herald. Fetch King Teethgrit an ale THIS INSTANT! And chocolates, please; plenty of them.'

The herald bowed and departed.

'I'm so sorry for this inconvenience, Your Majesty,' Vortas went on. 'Please do tell me what happened.'

Groan shrugged. 'We go' in a candle shop an' the ol' girl in there did for us.'

'I see. And may I ask why you broke into the candle shop, Your Majesty? I mean, presumably your visit to Dullitch has something to do with Viscount Curfew?'

'Yeah well, we was on our way 'ere to do trade when Gordo – tha's me mate - said we should 'elp me bruvva out first.'

'What's wrong with your brother?'

'He's asleep.'

Vortas nodded. 'Yes...so I understand, but why are you unable to wake him up?'

'Oh, 'cause he smashed one o' them glass fings and now he's cursed.'

'I see. And you say you came here to do trade with the viscount?'

'Yeah. We've got an 'ammer he might want.'

'A hammer?'

'Yeah, some wizard used it to put up a shelf at the start o' the tri-age. S' a special 'ammer.'

'Ahh. Well, I think the best thing we can do is to put you and your friends in three of our exclusive guest rooms, and then you can speak to the viscount tomorrow. I'm sure he'll be interested in the hammer of which you speak, and I'm positive that we'll be able to help your brother in some small way. How does all that sound to you?'

Groan shrugged. 'Sall right.'

'Good. Then I bid you good evening, Your Majesty. It looks like your refreshment has arrived, now; the herald will show you and your friends to the rooms.'

Vortas nodded his head to the herald and swept out of the room, still carrying the scrolls he'd brought in with him.

'I like 'im,' said Groan, as the guards finally finished untying the old woman's knots. 'Knows a king when he sees one, that bloke.'

'Yes, Your Majesty,' the herald muttered. 'He certainly does.'

⁓

WHEN VORTAS LEFT THE HALL, he made straight for the kitchens, grabbing the first servant to pass him.

'I want you to go down to Mothal's Apothecary and buy up every anti-sleeping draught available,' he snapped. 'When that's done, I want you to give it to the page on duty and tell him that Mr Lythay wants the sleeping barbarian in the guest rooms woken up. Tell him to try *everything*, but to give each draught time to work before he administers the next.'

The boy nodded and hurried from the room.

CHAPTER
FIFTEEN

Morning arrived in Dullitch, and a sunny one at that.

Up at the palace, the sentry guard was changing shifts, the replacements arriving to don their armour for an event they all despised: the morning parade.

The parade was a daily occasion when all the guards gathered together, under their general and senior commanders, to fall in for the day. After the first ten minutes, most of the guards and the junior officers disappeared to perform their duties, while the senior ranks stood around drinking tea until they were called into the palace to sign the various forms and documents that would inevitably stir up rancour among their inferiors in the weeks ahead.

This time, however, their tea party was interrupted...by a giant cloaked in black.

The cart exploded into the open courtyard, immediately veered left and made straight for the officer's tent. The guards on duty, half out of protocol and half out of spite, headed straight for the palace to take up defensive positions.

Only a handful stayed, and those few not bowled over by the thundering horses, quickly got the general to safety as Nazz's cart careered into the tent.

The ogre reigned in the beasts as two smaller but equally masked figures leapt from the back of the cart and attacked the two stunned officers, reigning swift, pressure-point blows that caused both of them to drop like sacks of potatoes. Once unconscious, they were loaded into the cart, which was immediately wheeled around and driven back the way it had come; the two cloaked figures hurrying to leap on the side of it.

By the time the first troop of heavily armed guards arrived, all they could see was a trail of dust leading away from the collapsed wreckage of the officer's tent.

DEEP INSIDE THE PALACE, a page lifted Gape's drooping eyelids and squeezed three drops of liquid onto the pupils: it was the third such operation he'd performed in the space of just ten minutes.

And, still, there was no reaction whatsoever.

Nothing.

'There must be a powerful charm on you, mister,' he said quietly. 'I've thrown just about everything at you except Black Spyte...and I really don't want to use that because of the side effects.' He picked up the dark bottle, squinted at the handwriting, and read: May Cause Nausea, Increased Strength, Sudden Awareness, Pungent Flatulence and, in some cases, Death. Hmm...'

The page waited fifteen minutes, humming several irritating tunes as the time passed. Then he plunged the pipette into the bottle and administered the drops to Gape's eyes.

Nothing.

The page shook his head, despondently.

'Oh well,' he muttered. 'At least they can't say I didn't tr-'

'Agggggghghhhhhh! Heeeeeelpp mmeeeeeee! Agghghhhh!'

The page jumped up from his seat with such speed that he set off a nerve in his neck and collapsed in agony.

'Aghghhhhh!' Gape screamed. 'Get it off meeeeeeee! I can't taaaaaaaaaaaaaaaaaaakkkkkeeeeeee it!'

The big barbarian rolled off the bed he'd been lying on and, clutching his skull, collapsed to the floor.

After a few seconds, the page managed to crick his own neck back into position and plucked up enough courage to approach.

'Are-are you all right, mister?'

Gape opened one eye.

'Not really, no,' he said.

'Is there anything I can get you?'

'That depends. Where am I?'

'Dullitch Palace.'

'Fair enough; I'll have three steak sandwiches and a mug of ale. Oh, and some layer cake, if you've got any.'

'Of course. I'll get right onto-'

'Are the others here?'

'Er...I'm not sure who you mean, mister. I know your brother is here...and a dwarf?'

'That's them. Where are my swords?'

The page looked around the room and discovered the two longswords propped against a chair. 'They're right here, mister.'

'Good. I'm getting up, then.' Gape practically *leaped* to his feet. 'Ah...better. Now I'm going for a walk; I need to stretch my legs.'

'I thought you wanted some sandwiches?'

'Yes. Sandwiches are good...and some ale. After my walk. To stretch my legs.'

The page put his head on one side. 'Are you sure you're all right to go outside, mister? You look a bit...strange.'

'Strange,' Gape repeated, carefully. 'Strange. Yes...that's what happens to you when you come face to face with a god.'

'WELL DONE,' Effigy cried, as Jimmy and Obegarde hurried to close the yard doors behind the cart. 'Now get those two down into the basement of this house, and make sure you bind and gag them.'

'Whose house is it?' Jimmy enquired, looking doubtfully up at the high walls.

'It's rented,' Effigy explained, as the others dragged the officers into the building. 'And only for two days; the price was astronomical!'

'Yeah, well it would be in this neck of the woods: it's practically across the street from the palace!'

'Exactly.' Effigy scratched his wrist in agitation as the group reappeared at the back door. 'All done?' he asked, expectantly.

'All done,' Nazz confirmed.

'Good. Now, are you gentlemen ready to go?'

Victor and Mifkindle nodded.

'Very well: make sure you don't say *anything* until we're deep inside the palace. I'm taking the cart, albeit with just the one horse, so you lot will have to walk back. Jimmy, can you put the chains on them please? I'll do the same for Nazz, and then we're away!'

There followed a few moments of frantic activity, then the three prisoners were set.

Effigy grinned at them, encouragingly.

'You know how to slip those cuffs off, right?' he hazarded.

Three nods showed him that this was the case.

'Very well, then; let's move!'

'Good luck with your part of the plan, Effigy,' said Obegarde, shaking the freedom fighter firmly by the hand. 'I hope everything goes...with a bang.'

Effigy nodded. 'It will, my friends. It will.' And with that, he waved them on their way, wiped a lone tear from his eye...and rolled out the barrel.

DYING, it seemed, had done nothing to quell the ferocity of Rumlink Banks. The undead assassin paced about inside his cage, eyes reflecting emerald in the glare of the candlelight. When the door to the room opened, the creature stopped pacing and stood still.

The door closed again.

'Mister Banks, I presume,' said Diveal, emerging from the shadows. He put down the scroll he'd been reading and paused a moment to rub his hands together: the chamber had become very cold. 'I see that you were once a formidable assassin: one of the best, in fact.'

The thing in the cage stared back at him but made no sign of having heard the words.

'Never mind,' Diveal continued, stepping closer to the bars. 'The important thing is that you are here now and ready to do my bidding. All I need to do is clear your mind of all troubles, like this, and-'

Diveal paused for a moment; his attempt to delve into the creature's subconscious had failed. He tried again.

'Argghhh! Such hatred! Who is this young man you so despise? Let me see if we can turn your...argghhhh!'

Diveal staggered back, clutching his head, as the thing in the cage began to approach the bars. Its eyes were still locked on Diveal's, and it was smiling insanely.

'Back down, damn you! You're no good to me if I can't direct your hatred elsewhereaaargh! Stop it! Stop fiiiighting me!'

Diveal darted forward and slammed a boot into the bars, jarring the cage and breaking the creature's focus.

'Let's try again, shall we?' he muttered, glaring at the undead face once more. 'You WILL obey my commands.'

I will not, said the mind of Rumlink Banks. *I only remain to avenge my death. Then I shall depart this place...* Diveal increased the intensity of his gaze.

'YOU WILL OBEY ME.'

Never.

'YOU WILL.'

No.

'YES.'

A vein began to throb in the impostor's temple.

'YES. YOU. WILL.'

The creature's green eyes flickered, and it bowed its head.

I will, said the steely mind. *For now.*

THE VENOM OF VANQUISH

When Colonel Reish and Brigadier Lanslide arrived at the palace gates, they were greeted by a group of relieved (and very guilty-looking) guards.

'Sirs, sirs! It's really you! Thank the gods you're alive!'

'No thanks to you,' Obegarde snapped, trying to come to terms with the Brigadier's strangely melodic voice.

'A pathetic show from you boys,' Colonel Reish agreed in a not-at-all like Jimmy Quickstint tone. 'We had to tackle and arrest these three miscreants single, er, that is *double*-handed.'

The guards all looked at their feet.

'We're really sorry, sirs,' said the captain, ashamedly. 'It'll never happen, again.'

'Yes, well, it better not,' the Colonel finished, marching past the guards. 'Don't worry about these prisoners; we took them on by ourselves so we might as well go the whole hog and lock them away, too. You lot just get on with whatever it is you actually *do* down here.'

As the guards nodded and went about their business, Obegarde whispered to Jimmy: 'Unbelievable! You're actually enjoying yourself, aren't you?'

The colonel grinned. 'I might be,' he admitted.

'I might be, SIR.'

'Yeah; right.'

The two fake officers shared a smile...then turned and walked right into the general. Acting on instinct, they dashed off a quick salute.

'You're both alive then, I see?' he snapped, twiddling the ends of his tapering moustache. 'And prisoners, too? Good to see that all those years of training haven't gone amiss...'

'Yes, sir.'

'No, sir.'

'ABSOLUTELY SIR!'

'Splendid,' said the general, nodding. 'Well, it's very fortunate that you're back; you're both needed in my office to sign Lord Curfew's pledge.'

'Pledge?' Colonel Reish exclaimed, then, remembering himself, added; 'Sir?'

'Yes, yes,' the general went on. 'The pledge he and Mr Lythay have drawn up declaring him Dullitch Overlord. I don't know what it is with nobles these days; no title's ever good enough for them!'

'Overlord?' said Brigadier Lanslide. 'Does that give him extra dominion or something?'

The general shook his head.

'Not really,' he said. 'It just means that he no longer needs the council to ratify his decisions; not that they ever did anyway! Hahahaha!'

Two very dry laughs echoed the general's own.

'Still,' he went on. 'Overlord, eh? What a pompous title! Admittedly Baron and Marquis would have been a step back, but we offered him Earl, Duke, Prince and even King; he wasn't having any of it! Oh well, at least it's all sorted out, now. I just need you two gentlemen to put your paw prints on the bottom of the army's pledge to back him, then we can all take the night off!'

Colonel Reish and Brigadier Lanslide shared an awkward glance.

'No problem,' said Lanslide, before his colleague could cut in. 'We'll go and put these prisoners in the interrogation rooms, then we'll all be right with you.'

'Very good, gentlemen. I'll see you soon.'

The general turned and headed through a side door.

'So that's his plan!' Obegarde whispered. 'To get total

control over the city! He's already eliminated all the councillors that count, and now he's declaring himself Dullitch Overlord! What's next; Emperor of Illmoor?'

'Can't be far off,' Jimmy agreed, trying to keep the group moving in a northerly direction without actually having a clue where they were headed. 'Where are we going, anyway?'

'Up,' Obegarde confirmed. 'At least, until we hit the palatial apartments.' He nodded at salutes from several guards as the command group passed. 'I wonder how Effigy's doing.'

THE CART RATTLED into the palace courtyard and would have carried on regardless if two sturdy sentries hadn't immediately barred the path. Unfortunately, they'd learned their lesson earlier that day, and weren't about to be dragged before the general on a charge of gross incompetence.

'Oi: you in the cart!' one shouted. 'State your name and business!'

'Bunhilda's Brewery,' Effigy spat onto the cobbles beside the cart. 'Ale delivery.'

The guards peered into the back of the cart, which contained a single barrel.

'We've had an ale delivery this week,' said the second guard, doubtfully. 'Besides, there's only one barrel in there, and we usually get forty in a cart twice the size of yours.'

Effigy didn't miss a beat; he swore loudly under his breath, leapt from the cart onto the cobbles and ripped a scroll from his jerkin, waving it under the nose of the nearest guard before snatching it back.

'One barrel of Piker's Rum, to be personally signed for by one Brigadier...er...how do you say this Lampslater?'

'Lanslide,' the first guard corrected him. 'Really? The Brigadier's getting rum personally delivered now?'

'His drink problem's getting worse,' said the second guard, sagely. 'There's been rumours flying all over the palace that he's on more than a hundred glasses a day.'

'Smokes, too,' said the first. 'Like a chimney-top.' 'Er...excuse me,' said Effigy, feigning annoyance. 'Do you mind if I take this barrel through? Only, the delivery note says to have it signed for by midday.'

'Yeah, all right,' the guard nodded grudgingly. 'But one of us is going to have to accompany you.'

'Right; no sweat. Delivery note says it needs to go to the Summer Gardens...wherever *they* might be.'

The first guard nodded.

'They must mean one of the kitchen entrances,' he advised. 'I'll take you straight down there.'

'Great.'

Effigy unloaded the barrel from the back of the cart and hefted it onto one shoulder, trying not to wince as he realised the weight of the powder.

'Lead on,' he managed, following the guard around one corner of the palace's main building and into an extensive maze of grounds.

'This way.'

'I'm right behind you.'

～

OBEGARDE AND JIMMY arrived at the top of a long flight of steps, their prisoners still in tow.

'I'm completely lost,' Obegarde admitted. 'And I've been here before.

'Me too,' said Jimmy. 'I swear they change the place every year. You know, put in new corridors, switch rooms, and the like.'

'Mmm...I bet it's a defence mechanism,' the vampire muttered.

'Well, it certainly works! I've seen that potted plant with the banana-shaped leaves seven times in the last half-hour...and I'm originally a thief by trade: I can find my way around most places in Dullitch, blindfolded.'

Obegarde shrugged. 'Well, maybe you should put one on – it might help.'

'Er...can we speak yet?' Nazz enquired.

'No! Shhhh! Officers wouldn't fraternise with the prisoners who'd just tried to kidnap them! They'd treat them like scum...maybe even rough them up a bit...'

'Aghh!' said Victor suddenly, yelping at Jimmy. 'What was that for?'

'I was roughing you up a bit.'

'Yeah? Well if you do it again, you'll be looking for your eyeballs on the floor.'

'Hey, I'm just playing my character, here.'

'You'll be playing a dead character in a minute.'

Obegarde suddenly shoved the two men apart. 'Will everybody just be quiet! We need to find the private apartments pretty sharpish, or we're going to get found out. Agreed?'

'Agreed.'

'Good. Then shut the hell up so we can all get moving.'

'Shh! Look!' As they turned a sharp corner, Jimmy pointed at the end of the new corridor. 'There are two guards outside *that* room; whoever's in there must be pretty important!'

'Agreed,' Obegarde whispered. 'But, look, there's a chain post on the west wall: I think you two should stay here for now. Jimmy and I will go ahead and clear the way.'

'How do we chain ourselves-'

'Don't chain yourselves to anything! Just try to look as if you're chained up. Loop your hands through the post or something...'

That said, Brigadier Lanslide and Colonel Reish marched determinedly forward.

'Arrived for a trade deal?' Sorrell Diveal paced the room, his brow furrowed. 'What trade deal? I thought all the consortiums traded independently with Phlegm; they have permission to...'

'I could always poison him; it would need a lot and it would definitely require concentration, but it's certainly achievable...'

'No! We can't poison Groan Teethgrit: the man's an absolute monster; in the time it'd take him to die, he would realise he'd been poisoned and decapitate us all.'

Vortas frowned, suddenly. 'I thought you were immortal, master?'

'When did I tell you that?'

'The other night, when you told me your other...secrets.'

Diveal swallowed.

'Immortal is too strong a word,' he said, slowly. 'Let's just say that I have an agreement with some very dark gods who want me to run this city and...find something for them.

Vortas nodded. 'Understood, master. But, if we're not going to poison the idiot, what do we do about his proposal?'

'Hmm...tricky. A trade deal, you say?'

The poisoner thought for a moment. 'Actually, I think it's a personal deal; some hammer or other that he wants you to buy.'

'Hammer.'

Diveal suddenly went very pale.

'Yes, apparently somebody used it to put up the shelf on which Dullitch-'

'The Hammer of Romith: it was used to forge the Ledge of Medamichi.'

'Was it? I really couldn't say, master.'

'Hmm...I'll entertain him in one hour. Stock the meeting hall with your *special* fruits and ale. Oh, and have the fountains working, will you?'

Vortas looked momentarily doubtful. 'I thought you said I couldn't poison the King, master?'

'Don't kill him; just make sure that he's temporarily incapacitated.'

'Yes, master. You want him sent straight to the meeting hall, then?'

'No, have him brought here, first. I'll walk him down to the hall, myself: shows respect.'

Vortas bowed and slithered from the room.

'THERE'S SOMEONE COMING OUT!' Obegarde whispered.

'Don't worry,' said Jimmy, hurriedly. 'Just follow my lead.'

The two officers marched straight past Vortas Lythay, who was evidently in too much of a hurry to award them an acknowledgment. Presently, they arrived at the guarded door.

'At ease, gentlemen,' said Colonel Reish, authoritatively.

The two guards immediately relaxed, which was, they soon realized, a terrible mistake.

'Look at those shoes!' the colonel shrieked. 'I've never seen such dirty footwear in all my life! What's your name, private?'

The guard was literally shaking in his (admittedly filthy) boots.

'Private G-G-G'

'Never mind.'

'Get down to the kitchens immediately and shine those up!'

'But I can't, sir. We're not allowed to leave-'

'IF I SAY SHINE YOUR SHOES, YOU SHINE YOUR SHOES. NOW! GO GO GO!'

The guard disappeared like a magician; he even left his pike.

'I don't know what *you're* looking so pleased about,' said Brigadier Lanslide, to the second guard, stepping out from behind his colleague with a disgusted look on his face. 'Your breastplate makes his shoes look like mirrors! If you're not down in that kitchen before he gets there, you won't have a wage next month!'

The second guard vanished even quicker than his friend.

'You see how easy it is?' Jimmy whispered, motioning towards the end of the corridor for the others to approach. 'You just have to be *firm* with people. Now; shall we go in?'

'Knock first.'

'Of course.'

Jimmy rapped on the door.

'Yes?'

'Viscount Curfew?'

'You have to ask?'

The thief glanced back at Obegarde and grinned. Then he opened the door and peered around it.

'It's Colonel Reish, Excellency. I'm here with Brigadier Lanslide.'

Diveal rolled his eyes. 'I thought you two had been kidnapped...'

'Ah, no! We escaped, Excellency.'

'Very well. What do you want, then? Is this about the pledge you've been asked to sign?'

'Sort of, Excellency. But we've also got some prisoners we'd like you to have a look at?'

Diveal moved around to the back of his desk and sank into a large, V-shaped chair. 'Why do I need to see them?'

'Um...because...um...'

Brigadier Lanslide's voice cut into the room. 'Because they have a very unlikely story to tell and you just have to hear it, Excellency. They're claiming that you're an *impostor*.'

Jimmy spun around and glared at Obegarde as if he wanted to kill him. Then a voice from the room said:

'Have them enter. At once.'

Jimmy threw open the door, marched in and saluted. He was followed by Obegarde, who did the same, leading the three prisoners behind him.

Diveal, who was now sitting behind the desk with a concerned expression on his face, cracked his knuckles as the assortment of rogues trooped inside.

'Hmm...two murderous-looking youths and an ogre? You should have guards with you when escorting such scum through the palace; surely I don't have to tell you that?'

Colonel Reish shrugged off the claim. 'With respect, Excellency, we arrested all three of these villains between us, so I really don't think they're that much of a threat, do you?'

Diveal's lip curled up.

'Remember your position, colonel,' he snarled. 'Now, which of you three voiced this rumour; and why would you make such a claim?'

'I voiced it,' said Nazz suddenly, causing several of the others to gasp in alarm. 'And I claim it because I believe it's true.'

Diveal nodded slowly. 'And you are?'

Nazz sniffed. 'A friend of Burnie's is all you need to know, Lord of Scum.'

'Ah...so this is a rebellion of sorts, is it? Look, the troglodyte was-'

'-twice as brave as you?' Nazz nodded. 'Yes, thanks; I'd already guessed that.'

Diveal bristled with anger. 'How DARE you - I am your MONARCH.'

'You are not!'

This time it was Obegarde who called out, and he realized his mistake too late.

'Brigadier?' Diveal turned a stunned glance on him. 'What on Illmoor are you-'

'He's not *actually* Brigadier Lanslide...' said Jimmy, carefully. 'And I'm not, *in fact*, Colonel Reish; these are the very best disguises enchantment can buy. We have come to confront you, *whoever you are,* over the false capture of the throne of Dullitch and, significantly, over the disappearance of Viscount Curfew.'

'Oh really?' Diveal exclaimed, snaking his hand under the

desk and creeping his fingers towards the emergency bell-pull. 'Might I ask exactly who you people think you are?'

'We're the Secret Army of Dullitch,' said Obegarde, determinedly. 'And I wouldn't move that arm any further along the desk unless you don't mind losing it...'

'Threats...how interesting.' Diveal slowly got to his feet. 'Is there anybody in this room who is actually loyal to me?'

'I very much doubt it,' said the vampire, in a disgusted tone. 'Who the hell are you, anyway?'

There came the first sound of footfall from the passage outside. 'I'm the person who's going to make you bleed,' said Diveal, with a filthy smile.

The door flew open and Vortas Lythay strode in. He was followed by Groan and Gordo.

CHAPTER
SIXTEEN

'Ah...you are most welcome, Your Majesty,' Diveal said, hurriedly, as the group parted to admit the giant barbarian and his partner. 'And you've arrived just in time to help me resolve this little matter?'

'Eh?' said Groan, glancing around at the gathering. 'Wass goin' on 'ere, then?'

'I'll tell you,' Diveal went on. 'These *intruders* are claiming I'm not who I say I am. They've come here, disguised as my own soldiers, to overthrow me...which is a terrible shame, as I was about to do a very lucrative deal with you over a certain hammer?'

Groan sniffed. 'Yeah, well we got the 'ammer 'ere, so this lot can all stuff off while you tell us 'ow much it's wurf to ya.'

Gordo chose this moment to carefully conceal the hammer by shifting his belt around.

'We're going nowhere,' said Obegarde. 'Until the viscount takes off his mask.'

'I'm not wearing any mask,' Diveal snapped back. 'Want to pull on my cheek and see?'

'Oi,' Gordo shouted, waddling into the fray and staring accusingly at the officer. 'You've arrested my friends! Get your stinkin-'

'I know it looks like that,' Nazz interrupted. 'But, actually, Gordo, we're all together.'

'Oh, right.' The dwarf nodded. 'That makes things a bit...complicated.'

'Yeah,' Groan agreed. 'Seein' as I'm gonna smash all yer faces in 'less you get outta my dealin' room.'

'Really?' Nazz said, flexing his inhuman biceps. 'You and whose army?'

'Don' need an 'rmy,' Groan boomed. 'I just 'it folk an' they go down.'

Diveal suddenly reached for the bell-pull, but it was slashed in half by Jimmy before he could tug it; Vortas made a frenzied leap for the door, but Obegarde was there like a bullet, throwing him aside and slamming the portal shut.

'Groan, Gordo,' said the colonel, suddenly, as Jimmy had an idea. 'Look; I can't say who I really am but, trust me, we know each other! We had an incredible adventure once, long ago, and if I looked like the real me I know you wouldn't fight us. We're on the side of good here, and-'

'I'm on the side o' money,' Groan thundered. 'Don' care wevver I know ya or not.'

'But *listen*,' Jimmy pleaded. 'You really don't want to make trouble, here. There are two assassins in this room, not to mention a massive ogre *and*, believe it or not, a vampire. Just for once in your life, back down.' He turned to the dwarf. 'Gordo, please, tell him to back down.'

Gordo squinted at the colonel.

'Did this big adventure we went on have rats involved in it somewhere along the line?'

The officer smiled, very faintly.

'I think I know who you are, then,' Gordo continued. 'What're you doing mixed up with this lot?'

'They're RIGHT! That man *isn't* Viscount Curfew!'

Gordo's mind raced back to the Curfew-like corpse in the forest, and he frowned slightly.

'I've had enough of this,' said Diveal, drawing a long sword from his belt and moving around to the front of the table. 'Haven't you, Your Majesty?'

'Yeah,' Groan boomed. 'They can all 'ave it.'

'Hang on just a minute-' Gordo started, but then all hell broke loose.

Diveal was the first to move, lunging across the room at Jimmy, who leapt back three seconds before Obegarde knocked the impostor's sword aside and head-butted him. Unfortunately, the vampire didn't have time to congratulate himself as Groan grabbed him by the collar and threw him fifteen feet across the room...to Nazz, who caught his friend in midair and set him on his feet again. That done, the ogre destroyed an ornate chair by the fireplace and, snatching up the leg, marched confidently towards Groan...who cut the leg in half with his own broadsword, then tossed the blade aside and threw an iron punch.

Obegarde hurried across the room to help Nazz, but Groan's punch had the knock-on effect of sending both of them crashing to the floor.

Seeing that Nazz and the vampire were out of the way, Diveal jumped to his feet, reclaimed his blade and dived, once again, in the direction of Jimmy Quickstint. He was blocked en route by Victor, who used two triple-edged daggers to parry the sword. Diveal let out a scream of rage, produced his own belt dagger and slashed a line along the young assassin's chest. Victor looked down and dropped to his knees...which gave Mifkindle the opportunity he was looking for. The assassin came sprinting across the room like a determined leopard and crashed into his prey, propelling himself and Sorrell Diveal through the window and onto the roof outside.

'Guards!' Diveal screamed as he landed in a shower of glass. 'Attack! Help me! Guards!'

Mifkindle was on his feet in seconds. A blade in both hands, he somersaulted forwards and drove the weapon deep into the impostor's shoulder. Diveal let out a scream...which twisted and emerged as a cackle, while the resulting wound healed up before the assassin's very eyes.

Mifkindle gulped. 'What in the name of-'

'Let's just say I have divine assistance,' Diveal snapped, throwing up a hand to snatch his enemy by the throat.

'V-v-victor!'

'On my way!' Victor cried, dashing towards the window. He'd just put one foot on the ledge when the covered cage in the corner of the room gave out and Rumlink Banks erupted from within like the worst kind of nightmare.

There was chaos in the room as the undead assassin slammed aside everyone who stood between himself and his murderer.

Victor gasped in disbelief, but he didn't have time to ready his blade before the beast was upon him, clawing, choking and biting his way to vengeance.

For a moment, whirling fists and a glint of steel were all that could be seen of the pair.

Victor fought valiantly, but he was no match for the undead fiend, who drove his needlepoint fingernails into the assassin's chest and cackled with delight at the resulting scream.

Diiiiiieeeeeeeee, the creature's tormented soul screamed out, *diiieeeee*.

Victor reached for his knife, managed to find it, and thrust upwards...but Banks caught his hand and forced the blade back towards his throat.

Down.

'No!' Victor fought hard against the pressure of his former tutor's grip, but to no avail.

Down.

'Arrgghhh! Somebody help!'

But no help came; everybody in the room was engaged in hellish combat of their own.

'Agh!'

The blade cut into the young assassin's flesh...and he began to lose consciousness.

Revenge! Reveeennnggee is miiiiinnne!'

The creature brought the knife down in a final, fatal stab. Then it raised itself in a triumphant pose...and its head rolled off.

Gordo retrieved his battleaxe and bent down to check the young assassin's pulse...but he found no signs of life. When he looked back at the decapitated remains of the undead fiend, a dark mist was rising from the skull. Gordo assisted its evaporation by swinging his axe through it in several great arcs.

Meanwhile, out on the roof, a frenzied battle was taking place.

'Oh, I do so like to throttle assassins,' Diveal muttered, hoisting Mifkindle off his feet and holding him aloft. Sensing that no good would come of trying to break the impostor's grip, Mifkindle reached for his dagger belt and produced two thin blades, driving one into Diveal's shoulder and the other into his neck.

'Arghghhhhh!'

Diveal dropped the assassin and staggered back, but he was soon plucking the knives out of his flesh as though they were rose thorns, casting them to the floor as the wounds miraculously healed once again.

'You're going to be a t-tough one,' said Mifkindle, throwing a punch that Diveal blocked with comparative ease.

'You have no idea,' the impostor concluded. He closed his grip around Mifkindle's fist until the assassin let out a yelp of pain. Then he spun him around and hurled him from the roof of the palace.

There was a long, drawn-out scream...followed by a deathly silence.

Back in the palace, the guards had begun to move. Several flew at the door to the chamber, driven on by the frantic sounds of battle coming from within.

'Lord Curfew!' came the cries. 'Lord Curfew!'

The door began to splinter under the pressure of countless toecaps while, inside the room, the battle was building to a frenzy.

Groan had met his match; the ogre was blocking every punch he threw. Moreover, some of the creature's own punches were hard to take. The big barbarian decided to change tactics, and head-butted him instead, which turned out to be a dreadful mistake: Groan felt a sudden, terrible pain, and his vision was suddenly tinted red.

Gordo, who'd moved away from the window and now had both Obegarde and Vortas Lythay backed into a corner, swiftly turned to face the guards as the door came down and they poured into the chamber.

'Arrest everyone except King Teethgrit and the dwarf!' Lythay screamed, backing away as a squad of troops divided to tackle the room's many occupants.

Jimmy was thrown against the wall and knocked unconscious by a guard half his size, while Obegarde fought off three guards before a further four dragged him, flailing, to the floor. Fortunately for the ten guards tackling Nazz, Groan managed to land a half-decent punch on the ogre before they tried to drag him down.

'Where's Viscount Curfew?' said a bewildered-looking sergeant.

'I'm here.'

Diveal struggled through the shattered remains of the window. 'Right; listen up. There's a corpse in the main courtyard and, by the looks of it, two in here. Remove them all.'

He produced a handkerchief from his sleeve and wiped it swiftly across his sweating brow.

'I want the two officers arrested and thrown into the tower...and before you think to question me, they're *not* Officers Reish and Lanslide; they are in fact the very thing that they accused *me* of being: they're impostors.'

The guards quickly dragged the officers to their feet.

'Now listen to me,' Diveal went on. 'These two are to be watched night and day until their true identities are revealed. And make sure you put them in the *top* tower cell...for these are no ordinary criminals.'

The guard captain nodded, and the prisoners were escorted out of the room.

'W-what about the ogre, Excellency?' asked one of the remaining soldiers. 'Should we put him in the tower, too?'

Diveal shrugged. 'You can hang him, eventually; but I want to speak to the impostors before he is executed. That way, we can torture him if the others don't talk. I *will* discover who their employer is, even if I have to bleed it out of them.'

'Yes, Excellency.'

The guards did as they were told and began to haul the prisoners away.

'W-what about the King?' said Vortas, his voice heavy with undertones. 'Shouldn't we *tend to His Majesty's wounds immediately*, master?'

'Yes.' Diveal turned to Groan and smiled, warmly. 'Yes, of course. Then we can begin negotiations on His Majesty's proposed deal.'

'Yeah,' said Groan, who was easily pleased.

'Hang on,' said Gordo, stepping in front of the group who were trying to wrench Jimmy from the room. 'Do you have to imprison the ogre? Only, I know him and-'

'Your place is with your king,' said Vortas, staring at the dwarf, determinedly. 'And you'd do well to remember it.'

'Oh, I would, would I?'

'Yeah,' said Groan. 'Show me 'omage.'

Gordo turned to look up at his friend. 'I'll show you both sides of this battleaxe in a minute...'

'How dare you speak to your king like that!' Vortas yelled, seizing on the opportunity like a spider descending on a fly. 'His Majesty deserves your respect!'

'Yeah,' said Groan.

Gordo was bristling with anger. 'Show *you* respect? The times I've saved *your* life? Get out of it, Groan Teethgrit...if you think I'm bowing to you, you must have fewer brains than I estimated...*and I didn't aim high.*'

'Yeah? Well, maybe I'm bedder off 'vout ya.'

'Ha! Maybe you are! I'd like to see how far you'd get without me watching your back, you great oaf.'

'That's it!' Diveal shouted, suddenly. 'That's treason against a king; a sovereign! Guards, arrest this dwarf and have him put with all the others.'

''Ang on,' said Groan, as if he was fighting some great internal war with himself. 'He's me mate.'

'Ha!' Gordo shouted. 'Some mate *you* are, you knuckle-headed moron!'

Groan cracked his knuckles.

'Yeah, a'right,' he boomed. 'Lock 'im up f'ra bit; do 'im good.'

'What? What! Why, you stinking-'

Gordo's words ran out as he was disarmed and dragged away by the guards. When all were departed and the noise had died away completely, Diveal turned to Vortas and said: 'Very good, my friend. Now, please escort King Teethgrit to the Meeting Hall, so we can take a look at this legendary hammer!'

Groan frowned for a moment.

'Damn,' he muttered. 'I reckon Gordo might still 'ave it on 'im.'

Diveal smiled, but his face began to sag.

'No problem at all,' said Vortas, quickly. 'I'll make sure that the hammer is retrieved from his dwarf friend.'

'Don' 'urt 'im.'

'Of course not, Majesty. Now do follow me, and I'll get you some medical attention. Then you can pop along to the Grand Hall and enjoy a fine selection of my special fruits while you're waiting for us to retrieve the hammer.'

'Yeah; all right.'

THE VENOM OF VANQUISH

~

ONE FLOOR UP, the prisoners were being hauled away.

'Now listen,' said Gordo, carefully. 'I am Captain, that's CAPTAIN, of the Phlegmian guard; if you know what's good for you, you'll-'

'Shut it!' said the guard who had a firm grip on his beard.

'Fine, I won't give you the pouch then.'

'What pouch?'

'The pouch of gold I've got hidden in my underpants.'

There was a moment of hesitation, in which the rest of the guards and their prisoners went on ahead.

'You've got a pouch of gold hidden in your underpants?' the greedy guard repeated, his frown threatening to consume both his eyeballs. 'How much is in it?'

Gordo smiled. 'Well, if you'll let go of my beard for a second, I'll tell you...'

The guard looked doubtful but did as he was told anyway.

Gordo put his hand inside his britches and pulled out the Hammer of Romith.

'Have you got change?' he said, swinging it up into the guard's face. 'Oh...I guess not.' Catching the man as he fell, Gordo dragged him swiftly into a side room and closed the door behind them. He found himself in a library of sorts, with no other exits leading from it.

Hurrying across to the window, Gordo peered down at the palace's inner courtyard. No guards were milling around down there, but he did spot a familiar-looking barbarian.

'Gape!' he cried, flinging open the window. 'You're awake! Gape! Psst! Psst! Gape, it's me; Gordo! GAPE!'

The barbarian, who'd been sauntering mindlessly

around the courtyard, looked up with a distant expression on his face. Then, saying nothing very much, he marched up to the wall and began to climb the ivy.

'Hello Gordo,' he said simply, when he'd reached the dwarf's little window. 'How's it going?'

'When did you wake up?' Gordo snapped, rearing back when he saw the strange glow in the barbarian's eyes. 'And what the hell's wrong with you?'

Gape smiled wanly. 'To answer your questions in order; a few minutes ago...and I've seen a god.'

'A what?'

'A god.'

'As in...'

'As in a deity, a supreme being...and a really nasty one at that. Fortunately, I escaped with my senility intact.'

Gordo frowned. 'You meant to say sanity, didn't you?'

'Yes, that too. How's *your* day going?'

'Well, probably better than yours...but, listen, Groan's turned on me, er, probably on *us*...and now he's about to do a deal with Viscount Curfew for the hammer. Only *I've* got it. Oh, and according to these other folks I met, Viscount Curfew isn't Viscount Curfew; he's some sort of wicked, sorcerous impostor...and I've got a really strong feeling that he's going to kill Groan.'

Gape snorted.

'Oh no,' he said. 'We can't let that happen.' Then he burst out laughing.

'What is WITH you?' Gordo exclaimed. 'Did this god you met send you nuts or something?'

Gape shook his head. 'No, but I had to fight him off...and I think I'm still a bit...happy about that.'

Gordo narrowed his eyes.

'Fine,' he said, dubiously. 'Now, do you think you can climb inside? Only, my whole secret escape thing looks a bit obvious with you hanging from the window ledge.'

Gape nodded and scrambled inside.

'What about your enchanted swords?' Gordo asked him. 'Where are they?'

The long-haired barbarian rolled his eyes, then turned, leaned from the window and, holding out both hands, gave a shrill whistle. There came the sound of breaking glass as the two swords erupted from a window on the ground floor and flew across the courtyard.

'Thanks for reminding me,' Gape said, juddering a little as the two weapons landed in his hands. 'I'd forget my head if it wasn't both feet.'

Gordo looked at him doubtfully.

'Gape,' he began. 'I'm *really* worried about you. But look, just for now, I want you to stay close beside me and don't say a word.'

'Right,' said Gape, obediently. 'Where are we going, then?'

Gordo rolled his eyes. 'We're *going* to find Groan and get out of here.'

～

ONCE VORTAS HAD MADE sure that Groan was comfortable and had a constant supply of wine and chocolates, he left the hall and headed for the tower. He hadn't gone more than ten steps when a breathless guard intercepted him.

'M-mister Lythay, sir. It's the dwarf: he's escaped!'

Vortas rolled his eyes. 'Can't you people be trusted to do *anything* without supervision?'

'Y-yes, sir. The others are looking for him as we speak, sir.'

'Good,' said Lythay, sharply. 'We'll join them, shall we? After all, I want to be sure the hammer gets to His Lordship in *one* piece.'

'Y-yes, sir. Sorry, sir. There is m-more bad news, though, sir...'

Vortas stopped dead in the corridor.

'What NOW?' he snapped.

'Er...the other barbarian, sir: the one that was under the weather.'

'Yes: well?'

'He's disappeared too, sir. We think they were both seen upstairs a few minutes ago.'

'You *think*?'

'Yes, sir. The guard who saw 'em only has one eye.'

Vortas nodded. 'Terrific. Just terrific. Apologise to King Groan, and then bring him to Lord Curfew's office. I don't want this getting out of hand.'

CHAPTER
SEVENTEEN

'Oh great gods – a squirrel with a scimitar: look!'

The guard spun around, giving Effigy enough time to lower the barrel and strike him over the head with a leather cosh.

'Unbelievable,' he muttered. 'Oldest trick in the book, and still they fall for it. Now, where am I?'

Dragging the guard into a convenient bush and promptly returning for the barrel, he delved in his pockets and produced Shably's plan of the Summer Gardens. According to the hastily scrawled notes, the tunnel entrance was right behind him.

Effigy turned and examined the wall, but all the bricks seemed to be in place. He decided to prod each one to find out if there was any sign of give in them...and came up trumps on the third brick he pushed. The wall slid noiselessly outward, on oiled hinges.

Effigy peered inside the tunnel and listened for any sound of footsteps. Then he rolled the barrel inside and closed the secret door behind him. It was at this point Effigy reflected that he really ought to have brought along a lantern of some sort.

Still, the job had to be done...so he headed into the darkness, rolling the barrel ahead of him.

∽

'Escaped,' said Diveal, carefully, cracking his knuckles and looking the trembling guard square in the eye. 'How, exactly? He was standing in this very room not ten minutes ago! All I asked was that you take him straight to the tower and you couldn't even manage that? Why did Curf-do I-put up with you? FIND HIM NOW!'

'Yeah,' Groan added. 'And don' 'urt 'im or I'll rip yer skull off. 'Jus' get the 'ammer off 'im.'

The guard bowed and hurried out of the room.

'Now, Your Majesty, shall we move along?'

'Yeah,' Groan rumbled. 'I'm starvin'.'

∽

The infamous Tower of Torture housed the highest cell in Dullitch Palace. Obegarde, Jimmy and Nazz hung despondently on chains set into the walls.

'Magnificent view, isn't it?' Obegarde observed. 'Hmm...I wonder if they made the windows this big to show people how deadly it'd be if they "accidentally" fell out of them? You know, so they'll talk...'

'I don't believe this,' said Jimmy, resentfully, yanking at his chains. 'I mean; how can this be happening to us? Who IS that thing on the throne?'

'Who cares!' Obegarde screamed. 'It doesn't matter who he is!'

'Yeah, right,' Jimmy sniffed. 'We're all going to be hanged now, anyway! Well, two of us are; you're already dead!'

'Half dead,' the vampire corrected.

'I'm not waiting around to be hanged,' said Nazz, wrenching away from the wall with incredible strength. 'I'm getting out NOW.' He tried twice more to rip out the chains that held him, to no avail.

'You'll never do it,' said Jimmy, despondently. 'Dullitch Palace is renowned for the strength of its chains. It's pointless to struggle.' He turned to Obegarde. 'But *you* should be able to get out, no problem...and then you can let *me* out.'

The vampire looked up suddenly.

'Why should *I* be able to escape?'

'Well, you're a vampire aren't you? I know for a fact you can change shape; I've seen you do it!'

'Ha! Once a year, maybe; but it takes an *incredible* amount of energy, and I'm next to useless afterwards!'

Jimmy muttered something under his breath.

'Well,' said Nazz, evenly. 'Do you think you might be able to *try*? After all, it would be nice to think we had one tiny sliver of hope, after what happened to those two assassins back there!'

Obegarde sighed, deeply.

'All right,' he said, and closed his eyes.

Several minutes passed, but nothing happened.

'Obegarde,' Jimmy whispered.

Nothing.

'Oi! Obegarde! Pst! OBEGARDE!'

The vampire's eyes flicked open.

'What? What happened?'

'You fell asleep,' Jimmy screamed. 'You actually fell *asleep* while trying to save us all from mortal danger!'

Obegarde swore under his breath.

'I wasn't asleep,' he continued, glaring across at the thief. 'I was concentrating!'

'You were snoring!'

'Look, I'm trying-'

'No, you're not!'

'I AM, damn it!'

'Don't bother,' said Nazz, and heaved away from the wall with such might that half the brickwork came away. Then the big ogre padded across the room and tore down Jimmy's chains.

The shocked thief took a moment to pull himself together, then looked on in amazement as Nazz made short work of Obegarde's chains.

'You ogres are quite tough, aren't you?' he said.

SENSING the approaching end of the passage, Effigy Spatula lowered his barrel of Fumeback powder onto the floor and tiptoed into the alcove that marked the tunnel's termination. There was a bricked-up wall with two circular slots at eye-height; both were covered with metal caps.

Effigy dragged the barrel across the floor and propped it against the wall, then he silently reached up and unscrewed the caps. Light flowed out, and for a moment, he couldn't see anything but dust. Then his vision settled, and he saw the room beyond. He also saw its occupant, the apparent viscount, lying on the bed with one hand over his forehead. After a few moments, he began to wince as a seemingly terrible pain took him: all the while, his face looked odd and dreamy, as though he was struggling against some unforeseen magic in order to keep himself in order.

They were right, Effigy thought, *he's not Curfew at all*.

It was nearly time...

SNAP. SNAP. CRACK. SNAP. CRAAAACK.

Effigy looked down in horror at the pile of twigs he hadn't noticed strewn across the floor beneath the spyhole. Shaking with fear, he quickly peered back into the room...but the impostor was nowhere to be seen.

Effigy heard footsteps approaching.

He moved back and sidestepped carefully to his left, feeling his way along the tunnel wall in an attempt to locate a convenient alcove in which to hide. Unfortunately, before he could find one, the section of the wall he was searching swung outwards and knocked him off his feet.

'Ah...how nice of you to drop by!'

Diveal strode out into the tunnel, kicking the intruder hard in the face as he attempted to get up.

'Do you break into the palace regularly or is it just a quick job for a local consortium?'

'I-I'm a freedom fighter,' came the reply, as Effigy dabbed some blood from his lip.

'Ah yes? I'm not actually that surprised.' Diveal grinned. 'You see, I seem to have met quite a few of you lot today. In any other circumstances, I'd call for the palace guard, but from the looks of you I think I can probably handle this situation quite capably, myself.'

He drove his fist downwards, but Effigy managed to roll aside at the last moment and he glanced at the wall instead.

'You're not Curfew,' Effigy spat, sweeping the viscount's legs out from under him and sending the man crashing to the floor. 'You're nothing but a damned impostor and I'll rot in torment before a wretch like you sits on the throne of this fair cit-'

'Actually my name is Diveal,' said the impostor, rising from the floor with lightning speed and snatching Effigy by the throat with both hands. 'And you're quite right: I am not your pathetically incompetent ruler...rather, I am his murderer *and* his successor. Not only that, but as you can see I have this wonderful city that used to belong to the fool...AND his marvellous palace.'

Effigy struggled to break the chokehold engulfing him, but the impostor was far too strong. Instead, he decided to bring up a knee.

'Ahhhh!'

Diveal folded up and rolled onto the floor, just as Effigy managed to drag himself to his feet.

'I'm glad you like the palace,' he said, struggling over to the barrel and pulling a match from his jerkin. 'Hope you still like it after a few of my alterations...'

Grinning weakly, he struck the match and held it over the barrel.

'Fool!' Diveal snapped, his eyes widening at the sight. 'If you set that barrel alight you'll be doing me a favour: you'll kill yourself and you'll take half the gormless idiots in this building along with you!'

'Wrong,' said the freedom fighter, with a grin. 'In five minutes, the entire palace will be deserted.'

'Ha! Ridiculous; how can you possibly-'

Diveal stopped talking in mid-sentence: the fire bell had just gone off.

CHAPTER
EIGHTEEN

The fire bell chimed throughout the palace.

Guards rushed in every direction, trying frantically to outrun the general staff before the flames closed off all the entrances. Pages were shoved aside, cooks were trampled and maids were elbowed as the cowardly elite scrambled for a quick exit.

In the tunnel behind his private chamber, Sorrell Diveal gave a cunning smile.

'Insolent fool,' he said, rising to his feet and leaning on the tunnel wall. 'Your plan is ill-conceived. Didn't you think for one second that the guards would come to check on their lord and master before they vacated the palace?'

Effigy laughed.

'Not in this city, *lordship*,' he snapped. 'You'll be lucky if they remember you before they've had their dinner tonight.'

'Really? How irresponsible.' Diveal shrugged. 'Never mind: I'll reprimand them all in the morning...'

'There won't *be* a morning,' Effigy said, confidently. 'Not for you, not unless you admit your crimes and stand down from the throne.'

Diveal shook his head.

'I will do no such thing. I was *born* to rule Dullitch, just as I was *born* to discover the secret treasure of Illmoor. I have a destiny...'

'Secret treasure of Illmoor?' Effigy shook his head. 'I think you may well be insane...whoever you are.'

Diveal grinned.

'I've told you my name...and I can assure you that it is *you* who are insane. It is *you* and not I, who have come here to die.'

Effigy shook his head.

'No one needs to die as long as you admit your crimes and renounce your false ownership of the throne. If you refuse, on the other hand, we will **BOTH** be going on a long journey...'

The match went out, but Effigy was quick to light another. 'Are you willing to confess?'

This time, it was Diveal who shook his head.

'No, I am not. And you haven't the power to kill me here...'

Effigy frowned.

'You claim to be immortal, then?'

'Not immortal, but I am *blessed* by a higher power. By letting that match fall, you will kill yourself and destroy a part of the oldest palace in Illmoor. You're nothing but a fool; do you even know what it is that you're fighting for?'

Effigy smiled. 'Freedom.'

'And what's that? The ability to go off and wreak havoc in your own peculiar way? Ha! Do you know what a freedom fighter's ultimate fear is? It's that one day he might get his wish and have absolutely nothing left to fight for...Now blow out the match.'

Diveal snarled and began to walk confidently towards Effigy.

'Not one more step, *impostor*, I warn you...'

'Your choice, young man...'

'Yes, it **IS**.'

Effigy flicked the match into the air. Then he turned and ran like the wind...

~

THE PALACE WAS ALMOST DESERTED as Obegarde, Jimmy and Nazz made their way down the precarious flight of spiral steps that descended the tower. The noise of the bell was reduced here, almost distant.

'I can't believe we've only encountered one guard,' Obegarde muttered.

'Yeah,' Jimmy added, 'and *he* was unfortunate enough to be standing behind the door when Nazz kicked it through the stonework.'

'I hope he's all right,' said Nazz, concerned.

'Hah!' Obegarde cackled. 'Serves him right if he isn't: I've heard of guards falling asleep at their post, but never one who actually brings in a pillow to wedge against the doorframe. No wonder he didn't hear you breaking your chains, big guy.'

'Exactly,' Jimmy agreed, spotting an ornamental knife that was part of an elegant display on the near wall. 'Here, you're good with weapons.' He wrenched the blade from its clasp and handed it to the vampire, who secured it on his belt. 'So, where are we off to now?'

'We're going to get revenge on that impostor,' said Obegarde. He turned to Nazz. 'Do you think you can handle Groan?'

The ogre shrugged. 'Dunno: he's a tough customer. I'll try, though...if it'll help.'

'It will,' said Obegarde, cracking his knuckles. 'And I'll help you if necessary.'

'I don't know what's wrong with Groan,' said Jimmy. 'He's always been on the side of good before.'

'I guess he's just on the side of money,' Nazz hazarded. 'Shame, cause I really like his dwarf mate.'

'Yeah,' Jimmy conceded. 'Gordo's all right.'

'Shh!'

The duo came to an abrupt halt behind Obegarde, who had arrived at the bottom of the staircase and was peering intently around the corner, into the corridor beyond.

'Can you see something?'

'Yes: a few stragglers, but they're deserting. We need to hide out here for a few minutes, then we're heading straight for the throne ro-'

An explosion ripped through the palace: amid the deafening noise, half the walls on the east side of the first floor imploded. Obegarde flew back, crashing through the door of a nearby chamber and landing in an awkward heap in the room beyond, where he lay motionless.

Jimmy was more fortunate: shielded by the colossal bulk of Nazz, he crouched down while debris showered over them.

∽

'AGGHHHH! A BOMB! EVERYBODY GET OUT!'

Several of the palace officials were running around like headless chickens, tripping over each other as they dashed for the safety of the courtyard.

Vortas Lythay, halfway up the northern stairwell, spun around to find that his accompanying guard troop were still at the foot of the steps.

'What the – why are you still down there?'

The tallest of the ten guards looked around at the others before he spoke.

'Er...there was an explosion, sir.'

'And?'

'And we thought it might be wise to evacuate.'

'I see.' Vortas swallowed a few times and began to descend the stairs. 'Let me just remind you, gentlemen, in a vain hope that you have merely forgotten, that the viscount is still inside the palace. Your first duty is to him.'

'Yes, sir. Of course, sir. But-'

'May I also remind you that we have King Groan of Phlegm in our entertainment suite, a batch of disguised prisoners in the Tower of Torture, a rogue dwarf with a priceless artefact wandering the corridors and a missing barbarian who may well be with him. Don't you think that's rather a lot to worry about *without* running around like lunatics over some minor emergency...'

'Minor, sir? It sounds like it's taken out half o' the-'

'Silence! Pick up your pikes and follow me: we have enemies to apprehend!'

~

'I LOVE THE MOOOOOOONLIGHT; I love the moooonlight! I love it; I loooovee it like a moose loves the seaaaa! I love the moonlight, I love the moooon-'

'Gape, will you shut the hell up! What is wrong with you? Have you gone totally out of your tree? What are you singing for?'

The barbarian frowned.

'I was singing?' he exclaimed. 'Are you sure?'

'I'm positive, and I wouldn't necessarily call it *singing*.' Gordo rolled his eyes and peered around the corner.

'Did you hear that huge explosion?' Gape whispered.

'Yes! It's a blessing, 'cause all the guards are leaving now and we'll be able to get away.'

'What was it, do you think? A bomb?'

'I don't know,' Gordo admitted. 'Probably. Look, do you see those double doors over there?'

'The ones with the green stripes running down them?'

'No, two doors down from those.'

'Ah...the ones with the golden plaque outside...'

'No! You're looking at the wrong end of the corridor now!'

'Oh.' Gape peered around the corner. 'Then you mean the ones with the leopard-skin print nailed to them.'

'What?' Gordo squinted along the corridor. 'Where are they? I can't see any door with a leopard-skin-'

'Can you see a dragon egg?'

'No.'

'How about a llama sandwich?'

'Shut up, Gape, **OK**? You're obviously not well. So just shut up and follow me.'

'Fine...but if I get caught up in that lobster net, you can steal the treacle...'

'Yeah. Whatever.'

Gordo led the barbarian across to the nearest set of doors

and threw them open, hammer at the ready.

'What 're you doin' 'ere?' said Groan, rising from an enormous chair at the far end of the room. He had a bunch of grapes in one hand. 'I fought they pu' you in a cell.'

'They tried.' Gordo marched across the room and snatched the grapes out of Groan's hand. 'On *your* orders. Backstabber.'

The big barbarian sniffed.

'I would've come 'n' got ya 'fore they done torture on you or anythin'.'

'Yeah well...let's just get out of here, shall we? And what do you think you're doing eating their food? That fruit is probably poisoned up to the hilt!'

Groan sniffed. 'I don' reckon they'd try it; 'sides, I'm 'mune ta poisons.'

'Yeah, so you say,' Gordo muttered.

'You still got the 'ammer?'

'Yes, but we're **NOT** making a deal with the viscount.'

'Why?'

'Because he *isn't* the viscount; he's an impostor.'

'So? I don' care long as I get the money.'

'Yes, well, *you* might not. But I do.'

Groan sniffed again and rubbed his chin.

'Can' we just flog it to 'im an' then kill 'im?'

'No,' said the dwarf, dismissively. 'And it doesn't matter anyway; I'm sure there will be no shortage of buyers in Legrash and Spittle. Oh, and it might interest you to know that I found your brother.'

'Did ya? Where was he?'

'In the palace.'

'Ah,' Groan nodded. 'An' where's he now?'

'He's right her-'

Gordo looked over his shoulder, sighed, and then dashed out of the room. Groan picked up some more grapes and followed him, at a leisurely pace.

~

Vortas stepped into what was left of the viscount's private chamber. Three of the four walls were missing and the floor had been reduced to a series of wooden planks.

A cloaked figure crouched in the corner of the room, clutching its face.

'Master?' Vortas called tentatively, the guards all gathered around him.

'I'm hurt,' came the reply. The robed figure struggled to its feet, still clutching at the cowl. 'I escaped the full force of the blast, but I fear my face has been ...horribly disfigured.'

'Can you get across to me, master?'

'No!' The cowled figure held up a hand. 'I want you to find the hammer: it's...vital.'

'Yes, Master. But what about you? What if there is another bomb somewhere?'

'There isn't.' Diveal rose to his feet, pulling the cloak's hood down to cover all but his chin. 'I caught the criminal in his act of terrorism: he is dead now. But I need that hammer!'

'But what about the King-'

'Kill him! I don't have time to mess around any longer. Vortas, I need you to come closer. Alone.'

The secretary ordered his guard contingent back into the corridor and advanced carefully across the room's shattered floorboards.

'Master?' he enquired, crouching beside the figure.

Diveal turned his head slightly.

'Listen carefully; the hammer carried by the King's dwarf friend is no mere trade trinket. It is an enchanted key...'

'A key, master? A key to what?'

'That is not your concern, Vortas. *Your* concern lies in getting it for me. Now **GO**!'

The secretary frowned slightly but bowed nevertheless. Then he began to retrace his steps across the room.

'I will find it, master,' he called back.

A PIECE of masonry fell aside, and the rubble mountain shifted slightly. Effigy Spatula awoke. His ribs were on fire, his back was killing him and blood had begun to drip into his eyes. Still, on the positive side, he could see daylight beyond the rubble, and also, possibly, a rough outline of the palace garden.

Guards were rushing around like maniacs as various sections of the palace's rear wall collapsed. Effigy groaned with the pain and tried to move. He had to get away now. He heaved at the bricks around him.

Once.

Twice.

Third time lucky: several pieces fell away.

Effigy gritted his teeth and pushed himself up and out of the rubble. A lone figure staggering through the garden, he toppled a few times, trying to stay out of sight...but the guards, still attempting to save their own skins, couldn't have been less interested.

Effigy decided to take advantage of the fact and followed the steady stream of deserters through the palace gate and out into Dullitch.

~

'Not down there!' Jimmy snapped, pulling at Nazz's brick-like arms with all his might. 'There's a gang of guards around the doorway! Can't you see?'

The ogre squinted down the length of the corridor and sighed. 'But we don't have any choice! The other staircase is half destroyed and there's no point in going up when we're trying to get down.'

'Yes, but there's about ten guards down there, not to mention Groan and Gordo...'

'So what do we do?' said the ogre, motioning to the unconscious vampire in his arms. 'We're one man down, remember?'

Jimmy rubbed his chin thoughtfully.

'Dunno...' he began. 'Maybe we should climb out of a window or something. Do you think Effigy got out before the explosion?'

'Not if he *set* it off...'

'You're right.' Jimmy heaved a deep sigh. 'OK, now I don't mean to be rude, but *I'd* rather take Obegarde: otherwise, with you having to carry him, we'll all end up dead. *You're* the group muscle, remember?' He reached over and lifted Obegarde from the ogre's arms.

'That's stupid,' Nazz protested, sounding wounded. 'I can carry him practically without effort...'

Jimmy nodded. 'I know, but I need you to take out those ten guards for me.'

~

'Where ya goin'?' Groan boomed at Gordo, following the little dwarf up a long flight of stairs.

'I'm trying to find your brother!' Gordo called back.

'Do we 'ave to?'

'Yes!'

Gordo reached the top of the stairs and stopped short. Before him stood the snivelly character from the throne room, along with a gang of palace guards.

'We don't want any trouble,' said Vortas, carefully producing a dagger from his belt. 'We just need you to hand over the hammer before you leave the palace...'

'You want it?' Gordo reached down for the hammer, somewhat disappointed that his own trusty battleaxe wasn't closer to hand. 'Come 'an get it.'

Vortas smiled.

'Oh, we will,' he said, moving aside so that the guards could step around him. 'One way or another.'

It was at this point that Groan rounded the bend in the staircase.

Sorrell Diveal, still wreathed in the shadowy folds of his cloak, edged his way carefully around the floor of his collapsed private chamber.

Just as he reached the near wall, an immense figure thundered past the doorway. Diveal only saw it for a fleeting second, but he recognised the ogre immediately. The giant creature was followed, at length, by one of the mock officers, who was carrying the other, with difficulty.

Diveal smiled inwardly, stepped out into the corridor and sneaked up behind them. Then he coughed, very loudly.

CHAPTER
NINETEEN

As Groan stepped up beside him, Gordo hefted the hammer in one hand.

'I warn you,' he hazarded, with a smile. 'Groan and I have taken on enemies greater than you can possibly imagine...and we've always won.'

'Yeah,' Groan muttered. 'Thass coz we're 'ard.'

Vortas smiled from his lofty position beside the staircase and checked his pocket watch.

'Your luck might change at some point,' he said.

'Yes, it might.' Gordo sniffed. 'But not, I think, toda-'

Unfortunately, he didn't have time to finish the sentence before Groan collapsed in a heap beside him.

Gordo spun around.

'Groan? Groan! What's wrong with you?'

'I dunno,' said the big barbarian, confused. 'Me arms and legs 'ave gone 'eavy.'

'Oh, he's been temporarily paralysed,' said Vortas, giving a subtle signal for the guards to advance. 'Don't worry, though. He'll be able to witness everything that happens to you. Hmm...I do so love poisoning people. Now, if you'll just surrender and hand over the hammer, I can assure you that you won't be hurt...much.'

Vortas's smile rose on his face like a twisted sunbeam but abruptly fell again when Nazz appeared from nowhere and barrelled into five of the guards like a rogue cannonball.

'Oi!' Groan shouted, as the ogre smashed and crunched his way onto his feet. 'Get yer own enemies!'

'Just shut up, will you!' Gordo screamed, wielding the hammer and diving into the melee. Groan sighed and tried to move his left hand, but nothing happened.

Vortas, still watching from the side of the staircase, drew a thin dagger from his belt, and began to stalk the dwarf.

'Gord,' Groan boomed, pointing at the poisoner. 'He's gotta knife!'

'Thanks!' Gordo shouted back. *Where's Gape when you need him*, he thought.

∼

'CAN I HELP YOU, IMPOSTORS?'

Jimmy stopped dead in the corridor, and spun around, quickly dropping Obegarde in the process.

'Well?' Diveal continued, his evil smile expanding under the cover of his cowl. 'Are you going to make a move of some sort, *officer*?'

Jimmy spotted an ornamental mace hanging on the near wall and made a move towards it. Unfortunately, he was far too slow.

Diveal darted forward, glancing a single, powerful blow off Jimmy's skull and quickly spinning to deliver an equally devastating kick to the thief's midsection. As Jimmy reeled from the strength of the blows, Diveal delivered a boot-heel to the unconscious vampire's jaw and then brought the same heel to bear down on one of the creature's twisted wrists.

Such pain: he was really beginning to enjoy himself.

'Now,' he continued, looking down at both officers with deep disdain, the hood still hiding his face. 'Who shall I kill first? Hmm...you, I think. COLONEL.'

He reached down and snatched Jimmy by the throat, lifting the thief bodily into the air. Despite Jimmy's struggles, the chokehold was immovable.

Partially awakened by the blow to his jaw, Obegarde opened one eye and moaned slightly as the corridor swam into focus. There was Jimmy, being choked to death by the viscount's evil replacement. If he had enough strength, maybe he could...

Obegarde tried to raise himself, but one of his wrists was too weak and he collapsed back onto the floor of the corridor.

'Too late,' said Diveal, as if reading the vampire's mind. 'Your companion is no more.'

He released Jimmy's limp body and let it fall to the ground like a sack of potatoes.

'Well, there you have it. One dead, and one undead to go. Hahahahaha!'

Obegarde's eyes filled with tears as he saw the throttled expression on his friend's face. *Jimmy...he's killed Jimmy. Arggggggghhhhhh!*

He heaved himself off the ground with all his might, spun on his feet, and threw a desperate sucker punch at Diveal. It caught the impostor off guard, knocking him back, but Diveal's eyes shone like fragmented gemstones and he merely returned Obegarde's punch with a strength that took the vampire completely by surprise.

Obegarde collapsed in a heap...and he didn't get up again.

~

As Nazz pummelled his way through seven of the ten guards, Vortas advanced on Gordo with the remaining trio.

'He's comin' for ya!' Groan boomed. 'Watch 'im!'

'I am!' Gordo cried, waving the hammer threateningly and backing up at the same time. 'It's not easy taking on three opponents, you know!'

'I 'ad twenty o' them guards once!'

'Yes, Groan, but you're eight feet tall! I'm four foot nothing!'

'Just 'it 'em all!'

'Thanks for the advice, Groan. I really *don't* appreciate it.'

Gordo stepped back as the three guards began to circle him. Trying to feign an attack to the left, he suddenly swung right and slammed the hammer into the jaw of the nearest guard, who dropped where he stood and tumbled down the stairs. Gordo quickly turned back to face the others.

'Good 'it!' Groan shouted, trying with all his might to move the fingers on his right hand. He felt the merest hint of a tingle. 'Now do them uvver two!'

'I *am* trying!'

Vortas knew his moment was coming. He had to be careful; this dwarf was evidently a tough customer. Still, one accurate stab with his needle-blade, and the little creature would fall like anyone else...

He urged the two guards to move behind Gordo and stepped forward himself.

'That's it, little man...you can't watch all of us, can you? Eh?'

'I can try,' Gordo snapped, swinging the hammer in wild arcs whenever one of the guards was daring enough to take a shot at him. Then it happened.

Vortas lunged forward, Gordo dodged to avoid him...and the guards took their chance to grab an arm each.

'Arghhh! Get off me you...'

The guards prised Gordo's arms apart, forcing the little dwarf to drop the hammer. Then they held him up for the attention of their master.

Vortas Lythay beamed with sudden glee and thrust out the knife...which Groan knocked upwards, into the base of the poisoner's jaw.

There was a moment of incredible silence before Vortas Lythay's disgusted expression stayed with him forever. Diveal's most trusted servant staggered slightly, then fell flat on his face, twitched a few times...and was still.

'I 'ate 'im,' Groan pointed out, as the two guards sensed their impending doom and fled away like the wind. 'He poisoned me grapes.'

'Yes,' said Gordo, relief falling across his face like an avalanche. 'I think he probably did. Er...I take it the paralysis has worn off?'

'Looks like it.'

'Right. Then let's get a move on, shall we?'

JIMMY QUICKSTINT WAS LYING PRONE, faking his own demise. His eyes were rolled back in his head, and his tongue lolled sickeningly from his mouth. Unfortunately for Jimmy, despite his legendary acting skills, he could feel a sneeze coming on.

'Atchu!'

'Ah...' said Diveal, turning to grin at the terrified thief. 'Still alive, eh? How amusing. Well, there's no need to be afraid. This won't take long, I promise...' He snatched up the thief, driving his fist into Jimmy's face several times and causing a spray of blood to erupt from the thief's nose. The crimson liquid landed, in light splashes, on Obegarde's lips.

'Isn't this fun?' Diveal cried out.

He stepped back and, still grinning at his handiwork, raised his fist in a grand gesture to deliver the thief a killing blow...and paused, a quizzical expression on his face.

'What *are* you looking at?' he asked, turning to see why the cowering, beaten wretch was now staring past him.

He spun around...and a look of absolute terror settled on his face.

'Oh...hello,' said Gape. The barbarian had just walked out of the viscount's devastated chamber. He was carrying something. 'I'm just wandering through the palace. Isn't it lovely?'

Diveal was trembling with fear.

'G-g-give that to me,' he said, eyeing the glass orb that was pressed between the barbarian's hands.

'What, this?' Gape looked down, a stupid smile playing on his face. 'I found it in there! Finders, keepers, my dad always used to say. Besides, I really like these globes; they let you talk to the gods! Not that you can understand what they're saying mind, but still, it's nice to see 'em. The one inside here's really ugly, though: I think he might be *bad*. He was in the other one I saw, too: the one in the forest. He really got inside my head at first, but now I'm happy all the time. You know, because of songs and music. Would you like to hear a song?'

'I-I'm warning you,' Diveal snapped. 'Give that to me or face your doom.'

'Smash it!' Jimmy screamed at him. 'Smash it on the floor!'

'What?' Gape looked aghast. 'I'm not going to smash it! This is my favourite thing in the whole world...apart from my swords.'

Obegarde tasted blood; he began to lick his lips...feeling a terrible, desperate hunger for sustenance. His eyes twitched a few times and then flicked open. He could see the mace that Jimmy had dropped lying on the floor of the corridor and, summoning what little strength he had left, he reached out for it.

'I'll ask you once again,' said Diveal, his voice now edged with menace. 'GIVE me the globe.'

'No! It's mine. Miiinnneee.'

'This is your last chance...'

'That's a good name for a song, isn't it? Thiiiss is your laaast chance...'

Diveal dived forward, snatching hold of the globe. The two men struggled for a moment, but there was no way Gape was going to let go of his prize. Seizing the initiative, Jimmy Quickstint struggled to his feet and charged bodily into the pair. He didn't knock either of them over...but he wasn't *trying* to. He was trying to dislodge the globe from their grasp and, although he failed miserably, he *did* succeed in nudging Diveal off balance. At the same time, Gape yanked at the globe with all his might and lost his grip on it. Both men looked on in horror as the glass sphere flew upwards, and both made a series of desperate jumping grabs to reclaim it, but neither of them could reach up high enough.

Obegarde, on the other hand, leapt six feet in the air, kicked himself away from the near wall and swung out with the mace...shattering the globe into a thousand pieces.

Diveal let out a scream as if his very soul had been pierced...

CHAPTER
TWENTY

Nazz finished delivering a final devastating punch to the last of the guards and staggered over to join Gordo and Groan, who had recovered from his temporary paralysis.

'Are you OK?' Gordo asked him.

'I've been better,' the ogre admitted. 'But I'm doing all right, considering.' He extended a bulky hand towards Groan. 'About earlier; er...no hard feelings?'

The barbarian shrugged.

'I 'ad you beaten.'

'If you say so.'

The two immense warriors exchanged a knowing glance and shook hands.

'Thank the gods for that,' Gordo breathed. 'Can we go now?'

'Yeah,' said Groan. 'Member to take the 'ammer, tho'.'

The dwarf nodded, reaching down and snatching the hammer from the corridor floor. 'Right,' he said. 'We still need to find our weapons, which probably won't be easy in a place this size. You got any weapons to find, Nazzy?'

The ogre was somewhat distracted by a scream that erupted from further along the corridor.

'I think my friends are in trouble,' he said, and bolted off in the direction of the cry.

'Oh, great gods! Gape!' Gordo looked round at Groan, and both of them hurried after the ogre.

NAZZ, Groan and Gordo arrived in the centre of the passage to a grim scene: the two mock officers were standing over a decrepit figure, while Gape knelt a few feet away, clutching his head and mumbling.

Diveal looked as though all the life had gone out of him; his aristocratic air had been replaced by the snivelling spasms of the wretched.

'Murderer,' Obegarde growled. He'd drawn a blade from his belt and was advancing on the pathetic form. 'I don't know *who* or *what* you are, but you're a filthy murderer nonetheless. Now you'll pay for your crimes...'

Diveal's cowl had fallen away to reveal his true face, which was a network of ugly scars plastered over features that twitched with fear and malice. He looked utterly pathetic.

'P-please,' he managed, cringing. 'D-don't hurt me: I can't stand pain!'

The vampire grinned. 'Ha! That's always the way with evil despots, isn't it? They hate taking their own medicine...'

'But if I tell you *why* I did it-'

'We're not interested,' Obegarde spat. 'Save your explanation for the courts...they can have you when *I'm* finished...'

Diveal was suddenly cold; he tried to hug his knees for warmth. 'B-but it wasn't me! I w-work on behalf of another: a far greater power dictates me!'

'Rubbish.'

'It's true!'

'You will pay for your evil deeds, regardless,' the vampire continued. 'Now; any last requests?'

'I have one,' said Gordo, stepping around Obegarde and gently lowering the vampire's knife-wielding hand. 'You see, there are a few things I'd really like to know about this fellow and, if you're wanting to avoid another big fight...then I think you should leave him to me, Groan and Gape. We'll make him talk.'

'No!' Obegarde snapped. 'This man is an enemy of Dullitch. He needs to stand trial!'

'And he will,' said Gordo, evenly. 'But we've got some questions for him first. Surely you don't mind if he's...battered a bit when you get to drag him before the authorities?'

Obegarde started to shake his head, but Jimmy put a reassuring hand on the vampire's shoulder.

'Let's give them some time,' he said, glancing from Obegarde to Nazz and back again. 'Groan and Gordo are really good at this sort of thing and they've obviously got their own score to settle.'

'Damn right,' said Gordo. 'Nobody tries to imprison Gordo Goldeaxe and gets away with it.'

Nazz shrugged. 'Fine with me: as long as we get justice afterwards.'

'I suppose so,' Obegarde agreed. 'We'll give you half an

hour with him. Then we're contacting what's left of the council.'

Gordo nodded. 'Fine.'

'We'll be downstairs, mind,' Obegarde finished.

He, Jimmy and Nazz took one last, pained look at the crouching impostor...and headed off along the corridor.

Gordo waited until they'd disappeared. Then he knelt beside Diveal, drew a small dagger from his belt and brought the blade edge to within an inch of the man's throat.

'Who are you?' he whispered. 'REALLY?'

'My name is Diveal.'

Gape rubbed his head and even Groan had a flicker of recollection playing on his face.

'Sorrell Diveal?' Gordo repeated, suddenly remembering the tomb in the forest. 'The Sorrell Diveal who launched a fireball attack on Shinbone all those years ago?'

'YES!'

'Were you working on behalf of a higher power *then*?'

Diveal shrank back. 'Yes; myself and one other: Lord Sapp. We'd both studied dark magic since we were at Crestwell together. Then Shelmeth Ozryk, another lord, found us out. He told the High Council, who decided that we should never be given the chance to rule *even though we were first in line*. So we poisoned Ozryk, deserted the school, and wandered in the wilderness for a time. Oh, we knew it was wrong, but the power...was unimaginable.' A glaze seemed to drift over Diveal's watery eyes: it quickly vanished when Gordo put some careful pressure on the man's throat. 'P-please don't! I'll go on! Then, this one summer, when Sapp and I were walking in the woods near Beanstalk, we chanced upon a secret grove. There was a chapel, and-'

'We know,' said Gordo, tiredly. 'We've seen it.'

Diveal's eyes widened. 'YOU idiots destroyed the globe!'

'Yes,' Gordo confirmed. 'We did...and you're beginning to bore me now..'

The dwarf snarled and pressed his blade close to Diveal's neck once more.

'Ahhh...Sapp and I found the globes! There were two of them...and they contained the master's voice! He spoke to us both, and told us how to get what was rightfully ours!'

Gordo smiled. 'That's some bad advice, considering Sapp ended up in another dimension and you had to go into hiding after that botched fireball job!'

'Y-yes, b-but I took the globes with me and hid in the chapel for a long while, until the master convinced me to come out of hiding and claim the throne that is rightfully mine! He told me how to do it: the kidnap plot...but Curfew escaped and attacked me. *He* had to die. The master had already used his magic to make me look like Curfew...so he aided me again: he made Curfew's corpse look like me to sustain the deception. All I had to do was leave one of the power globes with him and make sure that the clearing was never found. I've been back to check on it many times since my...rise to the throne.'

Gordo smiled suddenly, his face eerie in the half-light of the corridor.

'Your master is called Vanquish,' he said. 'He's a dark god, isn't he?'

Diveal's face became a frozen mask of terror. 'H-how-'

'Because we recovered this hammer personally and we *know* about the prophecy...about *you* and the city. So tell me about this hammer...and WHY it's so special.'

Diveal began to shake with fear. 'I c-can't tell you about that-'

'You bedder,' Groan muttered, reaching down and snatching a handful of the impostor's hair. 'Or I'll rip yer damn 'ead off.'

Diveal was practically weeping with fear.

'You c-can't make me...h-he'll kill me.'

'*I'll* KILL ya.'

As Gordo backed away, Groan tightened his grip on the dishevelled figure and began to lift him from the ground by his hair.

'Agghghhhh! Stop! P-please! Agghgh! I'll tell you! I'll tell you!'

A sudden silence settled on the room. Even Gape, who was still trying desperately to get his thoughts back together, was momentarily engaged.

Groan lowered the impostor back to the ground, but, as he did so, Gordo again raised his dagger.

'TALK,' snarled the dwarf. 'OR DIE.'

Diveal put a hand to his forehead to stop himself from shaking.

'You know that Illmoor was originally a barren land of ash, and nothing more?'

Gordo nodded. 'Everyone does.'

'Yes...but not everyone knows that, before man came to dominate the land, it once housed two gods.'

'Gods?' Gordo and Groan shared a glance. 'As in, Thunder and Fire?'

'As in Good and Evil, Light and Dark or, in this case, Bobova and Vanquish.' Diveal sniffled. 'Bobova was the First Father of Illmoor. Having created men in his own image, he determined to build them a magnificent city, so he took up his magic hammer – the hammer you hold – and he carved a shelf in the Gleaming Mountains. Then he laid down the foundations of Dullitch, and poured all his power into making them strong.'

Diveal's mouth split into a nervous smile. 'It was around this time that Vanquish brought magic to Illmoor, choosing several particularly selfish men who quickly found reason to go to war over it. Battles raged between these warlocks and began to corrupt and shape the very continent...exactly according to the demon lord's plan. Well, naturally, Bobova was furious...and his form of revenge was to turn Vanquish's very magic against him, using a powerful spell to send him to a place known as The Dead Country, where – legend says - he became imprisoned...never to trouble Illmoor again.'

'Go on,' Gordo snapped, his eyes narrowing. 'I'm only half believing this gunk...'

Diveal shrugged. 'Well, after that, things went downhill very quickly. Bobova disappeared, his faith in men dwindled...and the warlock-lords utterly destroyed each other. Unfortunately, they also destroyed most of the good men and women Bobova had tirelessly created. In the end, only the secretive thieves and murderers were left...and it was *these very miscreants* who ended up finishing the construction of Dullitch.'

'What does any of this have to do with the hammer?' Gordo prompted, putting down his dagger and lifting the tool carefully from his belt.

Diveal looked suddenly very tired.

'Everything,' he said. 'You see, before he disappeared, Bobova built Dullitch Palace, and he made a portal which led from the throne room to...another place. He then put a spell upon the portal so that it could only be opened by a special key, which he gave to his son, Ramith.'

'The hammer...'

'Yes, but legend dictates that the hammer only *works* as the key if it is held by one of Bobova's own descendants – one of the blood – one...like me.'

Gordo spat on the ground before him. 'I doubt if Bobova would consider *you* a worthy descendent.'

'Maybe not,' Diveal agreed. 'But of all the lords of our generation, only Sapp and myself knew of the portal's existence. The rest were all ignorant of it.'

'So why didn't you try to find the hammer yourself?'

Diveal coughed and covered his mouth. 'M-my master told me not to bother looking for the hammer...he said that Teethgrit would bring it to me six months after I took the throne. My master, you see, is ALL knowing.'

'Your master is evil incarnate,' Gordo spat. 'And he'll never return to ravage the land while *we* walk it. Now, tell us what's on the other side of the portal?'

'Wh-what?'

'Bobova's portal; what does it lead to?' 'The greatest treasure in Illmoor,' Diveal said, his words crackling with excitement. 'The most spectacular and valuable wealth imaginable.'

Gordo smiled and gave the tool an experimental swing. 'Interesting; very inter-'

He hadn't finished his sentence when Diveal, sensing the dwarf's preoccupation, jumped up and snatched the hammer from his hand, kicking Gordo back in the process.

CHAPTER
TWENTY-ONE

'Are you sure we can trust them?' Obegarde asked, leaning against a corridor and smacking some dust from the heel of his boot.

'Absolutely.' Jimmy nodded. 'Groan and Gordo saved the city during the rat catastrophe: they're both solid. Besides, Groan is the king of Phlegm, now. If you can't trust a King-'

'But what do they want with him?' Nazz said, uneasily. 'I mean, they don't actually know him, do they?'

Jimmy shrugged.

'Let's just give them another ten minutes,' he said. 'Then we'll drag him down to City Hall.'

Obegarde rubbed his chin and nodded. 'If Curfew's dead...who do you think they will get to run the place? Visceral? Blood?'

'Nah.' Jimmy sniffed. 'My money's on Muttknuckles: the other two have enough on their plates with Legrash and Spittle, but Sneeze is tiny. Muttknuckles could easily put a mayor in there and take over Dullitch. It'd certainly be a step up for him!'

'Dullitch isn't a step up for anybody, though,' Nazz commented. 'Everyone who runs the place either ends up exiled or dead.' When the ogre looked up, his two companions were both quietly nodding.

∽

Sorrell Diveal might have been a snivelling wretch, Gordo reflected, but the man could certainly move when he wanted to.

Gordo hit the wall, hard. Groan and Gape both made to move, but before they had time to react, the impostor was halfway down the corridor, dashing toward the throne room with the hammer raised high over his head.

'Get after him, Groan!' Gordo cried, reaching for his dagger, but Gape was already way out in front.

When the three warriors arrived, out of breath, at the door to the throne room they found it locked.

'Ged back,' Groan warned, before delivering a kick that actually removed the door from its hinges.

Diveal had pulled the throne away from the far wall and was attempting to tear down the curtain that covered the stone behind it.

'Drop the 'ammer.' Groan commanded.

Diveal ignored him and started frantically clawing at the curtain, which was apparently refusing to budge.

The giant barbarian crossed the room in three successive bounds, cannoning into Diveal and knocking the hammer from his hand. The tool clattered to the floor and was quickly snatched up by Gape. Diveal toppled backwards over the throne but quickly got to his feet again.

However, he found Gordo Goldaxe waiting for him.

'Right, *now* you're beginning to annoy me...' the dwarf growled.

Diveal trembled slightly, a half-smile playing on his lips once again.

'OK,' he said. 'But look – just think for a second. The Greatest Treasure in the History of Illmoor – and all you have to do is let *me* put the hammer into the wall behind that drape.'

Gordo didn't flinch, but Groan was definitely buckling. He'd found a deadly-looking broadsword in a weapon-rack behind the door, and was slowly advancing towards the curtain, holding the blade out in front of him, a greedy smile on his face.

'What are you doing?' Gape shouted. 'We don't know *anything* about this hammer...it could be the key to something terrible.'

'No lock' door 'olds somefing bad,' Groan boomed. 'Only time ya lock a fing up is when you don' wan' uvver folk to get their 'ands on it...and that means it's worf somefing.'

'Don't be stupid, Groan!' Gordo snapped. 'Gape's right: we don't know anything-'

Groan lowered the sword. Then, with his other hand, he reached up and ripped the curtain away from the wall, revealing a scene that had been carved into the middle of the stone. The scene contained representations of a sun and a moon...but it also contained a hollowed-out niche in the shape of a hammer.

'You see?' Diveal screamed. 'I'm telling the truth; the greatest prize...Bobova's GRAND prize...and it's all yours! Just let me...'

'Why you?' Groan thundered. '*I'll* do it.'

Gape and Gordo both looked at the big barbarian with frank astonishment.

'Are you crazy?' Gordo spat. 'You CAN'T do it, Groan. You're not of the blood!'

'Then we let 'im do it...an' take all the gold.'

'And what if it's NOT gold? What if it's some special power that makes the first person that touches it immortal or something? How will we deal with this little wretch then, eh? Think, Groan! For once, just THINK!'

Gape said nothing but looked on as his brother's pained expression turned into one of revelation.

'Give 'im 'ere,' he boomed, padding across the room and snatching at the impostor's arm. 'What are you doing?' Diveal screamed. 'What are you – no! Nooooooo!'

Groan brought his broadsword down hard, severing the man's right hand clean from his arm.

∼

'Nooooooo!'

Jimmy looked up with a start, but Obegarde and Nazz were already making for the stairs.

'I knew there'd be trouble if we left them alone with him,' the vampire yelled back. 'You can't trust anybody, these days.'

Jimmy muttered something under his breath and hurried after them.

∼

As Diveal began to lose consciousness, a strangely disquieting smile spread across his face, Gape and Gordo made a joint effort to tie off the wound.

'What's *wrong* with you, Groan?' the dwarf screamed. 'Have you actually LOST your mind?'

But the giant barbarian wasn't listening anymore. He crossed the room and, fixing the hammer into Diveal's severed hand, drove it squarely into the space provided.

Unexpectedly, there was a low rumble of thunder outside. The room went suddenly dark.

'Groan?' Gordo called, leaving Gape to attend to Diveal's bloody stump. 'Are you all right? What's there? What's behind the portal?'

Groan remained silent, one hand still stretched out before him.

'Groan?' Gordo drew the belt dagger and slowly approached his friend. 'What IS it? Gold? Why has it gone dark in here? I told you not to try it! Groan!'

Gordo hurried up to the barbarian and put a hand on his shoulder.

'Groany? What's up with you? Don't tell me you've lost your marbles now – it was bad enough with Gape out of action! Groan! Answer me, damn it!'

There was a moment of terrible silence.

Then Gordo Goldaxe got his answer.

~

Obegarde, Nazz and Jimmy spilled into the throne room...and stopped dead.

Gape still crouched over the prone form of Diveal, but his attention was on the far side of the room...where Gordo

Goldaxe turned, his chest pumping with blood. He dropped his dagger and collapsed.

Groan Teethgrit stepped forward, upended his sword and drove it down after the dwarf.

'Groan!' Gape screamed. 'Th-that's Gordo!'

Jimmy Quickstint made to run across the room, but Obegarde, sensing the imminent threat, pulled him back.

'Let's get out of here,' he whispered. 'NOW!'

'I agree,' Nazz urged, quietly. 'We go.'

The three companions backed out of the throne room, then turned in the corridor and ran as fast as their legs could carry them.

Gape, meanwhile, having recovered from his own sense of shock, quickly leaped to his feet, drawing both swords in unison.

'Groan,' he said, sternly, staring in disbelief at Gordo's still body. 'Groan! Answer me, damn you: I'm your brother!'

A wickedly prescient smile bled across the face of Groan Teethgrit.

'I am Vanquish,' he said. 'Hear me roar.'

And then, there was nothing but the clash of steel and a few, terrible screams of pain.

Bobova's last answer to the greed of Illmoor had been revealed...

THE MIGHT OF MOLTENOAK

Vanquish has returned to Illmoor after an age in exile and none can stand against him. To make matters worse, the continent's greatest hero has become a vessel for the dark god's spirit and a relentless army of possessed zombies has been formed out of the mindless people of Dullitch. With nothing but a pitiful band of crusaders fighting for freedom, the cities of Illmoor are falling one by one.

Hope is fading fast ... And yet there is one - ancient and powerful enough to challenge the dark god.

Can Illmoor unite to face its greatest enemy yet?

COMING SOON

AUTHOR'S NOTE

I have included the following story as bonus material for collectors of the new Kingsbrook editions and I fully intend to include more stories in future books. The following tale - *The Dullitch Assassins* - has quite a long and celebrated history and it undoubtedly started my entire writing career. It was the first Illmoor short story I ever wrote, long before it occurred to me to turn the series into full-length novels. I sat down to write *The Dullitch Assassins* one Sunday afternoon in late 1996 when I was eighteen years old and still very new to the form. When I finished it, I promptly sent it off to the small-press magazine Xenos and got a letter from the editors praising the story but requesting a rewrite. Two rewrites later, it was accepted and published in the April edition of the magazine. It was then taken for reprinting in the professional international anthology Knights of Madness, whose editor - veteran anthologist, Peter Haining - decided it would close the collection that Terry Pratchett had opened with *Hollywood Chickens*. The anthology was published in the UK by Souvenir Press and Orbit Books and in the USA by

Penguin. The success of the book ended up inadvertently getting me signed by Ed Victor Ltd and led to me becoming a full-time author. It was given a third rewrite in 2007 for Dark Horizons, the British Fantasy Society magazine, in a celebration of the tenth anniversary of the series. It can also be found in Curse of the Kingslayer, the official Illmoor short story collection.

THE DULLITCH ASSASSINS

If you could accept that killing people was a necessary part of the job, and that getting your hands dirty generally meant you ended up covered in your own blood as well as other people's, then you were going places...though - admittedly - via the morgue. The problem with being a standout killer at Crumb Lane was knowing that you were a stand-out killer among a hundred or so other death-dealers who probably hadn't had the luck or the opportunity to surpass you....yet.

Victor Franklin was a standout killer for all the wrong reasons. He'd passed his first exam because Beau Bledling had fallen backwards out of a window, he'd aced his second final because Peacock Legrand couldn't hold his poison, and he'd scraped through the third with a critical victory over Beth Paison which had more to do with her gammy leg than his ability to spot a lurking patch of quicksand.

As far as he was concerned, Victor Franklin had never killed anybody. However, all that was about to change. If

Victor didn't kill someone this evening, there would be no windows, no poisons, no quicksand. There would just be death, and this time...the icy fingers wouldn't be touching anyone else.

Victor swung his left leg over the cemetery wall and dropped into the darkness beyond. So far so good, he reasoned, although fully aware that the worst was yet to come. Silence had settled on Dullitch Church like flies on excrement and thick swirling mists meandered between the gravestones.

A gorse bush provided ample cover as the young assassin fought with the clasp on his backpack. After a few mild curses, he produced the grappling hook and, stowing the pack away for collection later, crept towards the menacing shadows of the church. This, according to his friend Mifkindle, was the most important part of the test. Mifkindle Green was a fellow assassin at the school in Crumb Lane and shared most of Victor's classes: he had amazingly good luck and had drawn the relatively lenient Professor Crutchluddle for his last exam. Crutchluddle was partially blind and had one leg, not an ideal candidate for 'Dead Man's Boots', as the old man would have been first to admit. Mifkindle had disposed of the ancient master with apparent ease, finishing his final in a little under twenty minutes...including the time it took him to read the wrinkly git his last rights and order a plate of stew for supper.

Victor, on the other hand, had drawn poison-master Rumlink Banks for his graduation block. He knew students who would slice off their own heads rather than sign up for a final against Rumlink. The man had a reputation for being slippery as an eel and twice as fast. He had poisoned just about every prominent assassin in the school's history and was feared by students and teachers alike. Even the school's headmaster avoided Rumlink, and he was a strangler with more than fifty kills to his name. Victor had nearly lapsed into a fit of self-mutilation when he saw the examiner's signature printed on the small slip of paper beneath his own scrawl. He remembered thinking how typical it was that he should draw the most vicious rat in the pack. He had about as much chance of winning the Vanishing Village Olympics as he had of topping Rumlink this evening, especially on the man's favourite hunting ground. He'd been tracking the wily veteran for the past four hours, in some of the most appalling weather conditions ever experienced this side of the Gleaming Mountains. A sensible student would have given up by now, headed back to the schoolhouse and prayed fervently that his death would come swiftly in the night. Well, not Victor. He didn't know the meaning of the word 'quit'. This was partly because the men in his family tended towards insane bravery but mostly because none of them could read.

Out of the corner of his eye, Victor glimpsed a slight movement beyond the large stone cross that commemorated the legendary battle of Q'harm Forest. He crouched close to the ground, employing a low-level crawl to advance his movement. The area previously of interest was now silent, but it was the silky smooth silence created by someone proceeding with extreme care. Victor's gloved hand slipped to his belt and returned with an Orpal throwing knife, which he placed neatly between clenched teeth. He could still taste blood on the shaft; the result of a minor dispute but one that had cost him most of one finger.

Suddenly, and with almost shadow-like dexterity, a cloaked silhouette moved between the monuments. Victor dived behind the north face of the war memorial and gasped for breath as a poison-tipped dagger thudded into a tree stump, mere inches from his left leg. The young student allowed himself a brief exhalation of breath, confident in the knowledge that he had successfully earned a point in the 'close-but-no-cigar' column of his personal survival book: a habit he was determined not to break.

After a few seconds of frantic fumbling in the recesses of his right sock, Victor produced a small mirror securely attached to a thin stick which he unfolded before sliding the instrument along the ground beside him. When it appeared to be in the correct position, he employed a quick wrist movement to adjust the device at a right angle to the path. Unfortunately, the only object of interest in the resulting view was a similar device protruding from a marble statue, twelve feet away.

The two mirrors faced each other for a few seconds before both were quickly withdrawn.

Victor retrieved his stick and moved surreptitiously around the perimeter of the monument, his gaze not leaving the opposite stone for a second. Subconsciously he was aware that he now had the mental advantage, Rumlink finally having disclosed his shadowy presence. The sneaky old rat must have been fairly confident of his knife achieving the desired target. Ha! Take that and plant it, you vicious little skunkviper. Victor sighed; perhaps there was hope for him yet.

Making sure that every step was accurately revised, the student advanced along the grass verge, cold steel remaining tightly clenched between his teeth. He nearly swallowed the blade when Rumlink leaped from his hiding place like a prancing deer and crossed the verge at a dead run. Victor had to admit that the teacher moved extremely stealthily for a man of his age. He took a few seconds to wonder exactly what age this was, before remembering himself and sprinting off in pursuit. Even though Victor was some twenty seconds behind him, he could see that Rumlink's preferred destination was clear. The poison master was heading for the church itself. Once inside, the maze of chapels and bell towers would render tracking the wily veteran virtually impossible. Dullitch was a large church, large in the true sense of the word; the crypt was so well hidden that people died looking for it. Victor had no choice; he would have to dispose of the adept Mr. Banks before he reached the building.

He grabbed the knife from his mouth and accelerated his speed, clearing small bushes and low headstones in a complex series of leaps and bounds that would have injured a shorter boy for life. He saw Rumlink struggling (apparently without success) with the church's large double doors. Slowing slightly as he neared his target, Victor took aim and cast his dagger: the blade embedded itself in the back of the portal, about three inches from Rumlink's ear.

Hot damn.

Finally forcing the reluctant entrance, Rumlink took advantage of the careless shot and disappeared into the stygian darkness behind the door. Amidst sudden disappointment and confusion, Victor lost his footing and crashed to the ground, quickly curling into a foetal position to protect his head from any stray daggers. None came.

Allowing a few minutes to pass before attempting any sort of pursuit, Victor collected his thoughts and reached into his chest pocket for the Arlington Brassey blowpipe he always kept there. Keeping one eye firmly focused on the church entrance, he located his neck pouch and pulled a small, yellow-feathered, acid-tipped dart from within. He loaded up the pipe, flipped the safety cap over to cover the exposed hole and stepped cautiously forward.

The church door creaked open ominously on rusty hinges. So much for a stealthy entrance, Victor thought bitterly as he peered around the wooden portal. The entrance hall was deserted, with only a single candle to assist its meagre light, illuminating the immediate area only. Rumlink must already be in the main section, waiting patiently for his prey.

Victor plucked the flickering candle from its resting place, quickly stepping aside as a large black cat scurried out from under a desk to his left. Steeling his nerves, the student assassin applied gentle pressure to the inner door, forcing it ajar just enough to get a clear view of the east wing. The pews were empty but candlelight was plenty here, the elegant holders stretching the length of the aisles, almost three stands to a row. At least it wouldn't be a case of 'Blind Man's Bluff'. Victor had known many a pupil whose test had ended in that scenario; usually by judging the angle from which they had been stabbed in the neck. Life was not kind to the trainee assassins; short, but not kind.

Increasing pressure on the creaking oak enabled a more focused view of the centre aisles, and Victor flipped open the tube cap as he caught sight of Rumlink crouching down beside the altar. With a turn of speed that surprised himself as much as his tutor, the apprentice dived from the entrance portal and landed neatly behind the rear pew of the centre row. He heard Rumlink curse briefly as a lone dagger thudded into the stuffed model of an eagle suspended above the door, behind him. Badly judged, Victor mused. Perhaps the old snake was panicking.

That's two shots you've missed now, granddad.

He crawled, on his belly, to the edge of the pew and grabbed a prayer cushion, thrusting it out experimentally. A blue-tipped dart wedged into it. Make that three. Ah, the lethal master was already resorting to Gantolin.

As head of poison-related studies at the Crumb Lane School for Professional Killers, Rumlink Banks had known the properties of many poisons considered foreign to other masters. Usually, he introduced all his new finds to the staff; on occasions quite personally. This procedure did not apply to the use of Gantolin, Banks' own brainchild.

Gantolin consisted of the blood of the Gallows frog and the urine of the Prolonged Bird, one of the saddest creatures in existence. These were distilled using methods employed only by Banks himself until the resulting substance transformed into a light blue powder, perfect for dart tips. The effect of having this poison injected into the system was immediate paralysis, during which time you would generally be dispatched by knife or, if you were lucky, suffocation.

Victor quickly reached out and plucked the dart from the prayer cushion, hoping to employ it later, to his own benefit. Then, placing both hands firmly on the edge of the pew, he peered carefully over at the altar. Rumlink was reloading his blowpipe. Needing no further encouragement, the young assassin put the black tube to his lips and blew, sending a red blur across the church at his superior. There was a brief (but strangely unsatisfying) yelp and then, silence. Victor waited. Nothing.

Slowly, employing as much caution as excitement would allow, he ventured a glance back towards the altar. A single boot was visible from behind the steps. Victor wondered if there was a foot in it. Only one way to find out.

Slipping into the shadows of the seat wing, he proceeded towards the appendage, another dagger drawn and posed to strike. He was almost upon his destination when memory invaded his subconscious and metaphorically tapped him on the shoulder. The 'dead-boot', of course! The oldest trick in the book and Victor had nearly swallowed the bait. You approached the (supposedly) inanimate corpse and found just an empty boot, which you were bound to grab out of curiosity alone. That harmless-looking piece of leather footwear was (unbeknownst to the approaching enemy) filled with Opiolk Six, a poison so deadly that even inhaling its alluring aroma could paralyse the average man. Victor hesitated. While he never liked to think of himself as average, he had a sense of strange foreboding and firmly decided against advancement in his current line of inquiry. He had to find another route of approach, but how?

The young assassin quickly shook himself from his reverie when he noticed that he was absentmindedly playing with his bottom lip while humming a tune he had heard during a tavern dance at the weekend. He had to pull himself together, there was always a chance that his mentor had survived the dart and was watching him carefully from somewhere near the pulpit, waiting to take him out. Height, that was what he required; a position of technical brilliance from which he could view the entire chamber while remaining concealed himself. Slowly, carefully, his wandering eyes scaled the walls of the church interior, finally coming to rest on the creaking beams that supported the roof.

Victor cursed himself when he realised a serious mistake.

In the confusion of pursuing the old master, he had mislaid his grappling irons! There was no practical alternative, he would have to tackle the wall himself. Damn this assignment, it was tantamount to physical labour! After failing to spot a single feature of the wall that might double as a foothold, Victor settled on leaping from one of the pews in the left row nearest the door. Thirty seconds later the young assassin hung from the jutting nose of a particularly menacing gargoyle that occupied the gallery above. Offering silent praises to Sirlgynflinnexumemumannany (an extremely difficult deity to pray to), Victor swung back and forth for a few moments before building up the momentum to vault over the parapet and into the shadows beyond. Catching breath and regaining balance, he raced along the gallery towards his predefined vantage point, pausing briefly to check for any movement from the silent expanse of darkness below.

Nothing.

Victor reached the corner of the parapet, leaned out over a statue of Ohnmix the Everlasting in her incarnation as a buffalo ant and craned his neck for a better view of the altar. The boot remained inanimate but no foot protruded; it was a trap...and Banks was still alive. A shiver of uncertainty ran along the length of his spine and Victor quietly retracted into the bowels of the gallery. Now, everything seemed alive. Tapestries with travelling eyes explored his every movement, gargoyles blinked as he passed and attempted to grab him with awkward, incapable limbs. Victor admonished his wild imagination and prepared a mental summary of the many possible locations of concealment that the building offered to a fully trained and equally adept master of deception. Probably twice the number of hiding places available to the average apprentice, he surmised grudgingly.

Victor examined a few of the stacks, eventually pausing by an old piano to blow the thick overcoat of dust from a big blue hardback that perched jauntily on the lid. He squinted in the half-dark, just recognising the title. It was Lady Shapperley's Lurker by Maurice Kozlowski...a book his mother had once band him from reading as she felt strongly that a scene involving Lady Shapperly and the moth-faced incubus was disturbing. Victor suppressed a juvenile giggle as he successfully recalled sneaking out into the garden and reading the book behind the family's decrepit wishing well.

There was no obvious exit from the chamber apart from the portal through which he had entered, but this didn't fool the young assassin. Churches were notorious for all manner of trapdoors, priest-holes, sliding panels and rotating walls; besides which, there was a distinct chill on his back. He turned round to face a sturdy-looking bookcase with a difference that set it firmly apart from the other items of furniture strewn around the room; there were no books piled on top of it.

Victor crossed the decorative flagstones and scrutinised the old wooden construction. It stood approximately two inches away from the wall and was obviously concealing the source of the breeze that currently occupied the vestibule. Throwing all his weight against the oak monstrosity, Victor pushed the bookcase along the wall, noticing two important and valuable points in the process. Firstly, the fact that the case was as light as a feather because all the books inside were simply painted deceptions and consequently, all were glued in place. Secondly, there were handles adorning the inward-facing side of the case giving Victor the distinct impression that it had been left ajar on purpose.

Remembering his lessons in tactical illusion, Victor returned to the corridor outside and began to search for further access to the roof. When the fourteenth wall panel offered no secret mechanisms or sliding tendencies, Victor decided to ascend to the bell tower from outside the building. A decision he was fairly certain that Mr. Banks would not be expecting.

Seventy feet above the gravel drive of Dullitch Church, Victor clung to the concrete neck of a grimacing gargoyle and wished, quite fervently, that he were dead. Being the last in a long line of vertigo sufferers did not equip the assassin well for the task assigned to him by his own quick-thinking stupidity. Employing a smile of grim determination, the apprentice swung round with his legs, twisted his upper body and landed atop the statue, straddling the stone beast like a jockey. Then, gripping the creature's ears for leverage, he took the whole of his body weight onto his forearms and hoisted his lithe frame to a standing position atop the head, quickly snatching the guttering to regain his balance. Cautiously, he peered over the roof of the church. Banks was squatting just above the trapdoor which led down into the vestibule, obviously expecting him to emerge at any moment. Perhaps the master was not as cunning as his reputation promised. Victor reached down, his tongue clenched between his teeth as an aid to silence, and produced a short, stout dagger from his belt pouch. He tightened his fist around the handle and jammed it hard into the brick wall, beneath the guttering.

Using the embedded dagger as a foothold, Victor balanced on his left leg and swung his right onto the roof, gripping a handy metal rail that was wedged just above the slate for a purpose Victor couldn't imagine under the circumstances. He pulled a long, needle-thin stiletto from his foot strap and proceeded. The teacher appeared to remain blissfully unaware of his student's stealthy approach until the young assassin was almost upon him. Then, with surprising agility for a man of his girth, Banks dived aside as Victor lunged with his blade. With a deft sweeping motion, the master swept the young assassin's legs from beneath him, sending Victor crashing to the slate. The apprentice let out a yelp of pain but managed to roll swiftly aside as Banks brandished a gleaming dagger and steadied himself for the duel. He noticed that his opponent was limping and offered Victor a malicious grin, displaying two rows of dingy, yellow-stained teeth. When his junior produced no weapon, Banks perceived this a fatal miscalculation of need and darted forward. He was inches away from Victor when he lost his footing on the slates and staggered.

The trainee assassin spotted his momentary advantage and went in for the kill. Disregarding his now acute vertigo, Victor cleared a miniature steeple and careered into his mentor. The two figures crashed to the slate and somersaulted over one another, each in a desperate attempt to gain possession of the single dagger which Victor brandished over Rumlink Banks, teeth clenched in grim determination. The slanted roof gave way to a short space of levelled tiles over the vestry where the two men slowed to a halt and Rumlink finally managed to remove his aggressor by kicking hard against the student with both feet. Victor regained his footing quickly and moved the blade in a severe arc, describing Robis' Fourth Syllabus in the cold evening air. The teacher leaped to his feet and produced a similar stiletto from a breast pocket.

They circled warily, meeting in quick succession to the accompaniment of screaming metal. Neither teacher nor student uttered a curse at the other. Each man had the same purpose, no words would alter the situation.

Rumlink Banks' life had been fraught with incalculable risks. It was all part of being an efficient assassin. Professional killers often suffered numerous depressions and bouts of deep foreboding – death always did that to you. The most common characteristic of all true assassins was described by Reno Altiman, world-class killer, as the ultimate risk. The moment where normal men end and assassins begin. That fateful leap from a tower, the last grasping attempt to dispose of your opponent before he disposed of you. Every member of the school was given a lecture to this effect before signing up. It was designed to be the final deterrent for all but the most serious applicants. Rumlink was well aware of the ultimate risk. He took it.

Victor had never possessed the gift of anticipation. Mother Nature had simply never endowed him with the insight this skill required. Luckily for him, stealthy reactions more than made up for the disability. Rumlink, blade poised, darted forward like a rogue streak of lighting. When the master was mere inches from his prey, Victor swung round to avoid the blow with terminal velocity, sending the senior man headlong into the darkness beyond, waving his arms in a flail for mercy. Acting on instinct rather than aptitude, the apprentice quickly cast his last opal-studded dagger into the air after him. For a few seconds, seconds that he would never forget in his lifetime, Victor waited. He swallowed, breathing in frequent, desperate gasps. Slowly, he approached the edge of the guttering and peered over.

Rumlink Banks lay motionless on the church steps, the jagged knife protruding from his back. Victor winced, barely containing the overwhelming feeling of victory that was brewing up in his stomach. There was no doubt about it, the man had breathed his last.

Victor turned away from the scene and produced the pink slip of paper from beneath his belt. There was the space for Mr. Banks' signature. A pass in one of Crumb Lane's final exams was achieved by the absence of a master's signature, its presence usually indicating that the student had suffered a failure of no reprisal. Victor walked back along the roof and took one last look down at the corpse. He found himself wondering who would have the inevitable job of tidying things away. He didn't have to think very hard before a suspect came to mind. Candleholders smashed beyond repair; pews damaged and chipped. Still, he suspected it could have been a lot worse....

Shadow of the Shapeshifter

Vanquish Trilogy

David Lee Stone

CURSE OF THE KINGSLAYER

AN ILLMOOR COLLECTION

"..the natural heir to Terry Pratchett" SFRevu

DAVID LEE STONE

ABOUT THE AUTHOR

David Lee Stone was born 'David Lee Cooke' at QEQM Hospital in Margate on 25th January, 1978. He was educated at Ramsgate's Holy Trinity Primary School, where he spectacularly failed to pass what is now known as the Kent Test before proceeding to play truant at St. George's School in Broadstairs for most of the next five years. A solitary teenager, he decided to stay home and read books, a decision which soon led to writing novels of his own (and determinedly submitting them to publishers at the age of thirteen). Following early encouragement from his idol, Terry Pratchett, David made his first professional sale the following year, appearing alongside Terry in the comic fantasy anthology 'Knights of Madness'. To date, David has written some thirty books for many of the biggest publishers in the world, including Disney and Penguin in the USA and Hodder in the UK. Married with two children, he lives in Ramsgate. He describes himself as an undiagnosed autistic and a complete introvert who thrives on a daily routine that seldom changes. He can often be found tapping away at a keyboard in one of Thanet's many coffee shops.

facebook.com/kingsbrookpublishing
twitter.com/KingsbrookPubl1
instagram.com/kingsbrookpublishing